# HEADS UP

Fargo thought of something and lit down again. He returned to the thicket and selected a long, thin branch, using the Arkansas toothpick in his boot sheath to saw it loose. He sharpened both ends, then turned to the corpse.

"Turn your head, Wade, if you're squeamish," he warned.

"What are you doing?"

"There's a good chance those other three yellow curs are up there watching us with spyglasses. I figure turnabout is fair play."

Fargo carried a captured Cheyenne war hatchet in his saddlebag. He dug it out and made short work of severing Steele's head from his neck. He crammed one end of the sharpened stake into the neck stump, then anchored the grisly mess in the trail with the pain-contorted face staring up toward the rimrock.

"There," Fargo said as he mounted again. "I'm not one to mutilate the dead, but I want this bunch to see what happens once a man loses his head."

# THE TRAILSMAN

#358

# SIX-GUN VENDETTA

**by**
**Jon Sharpe**

A SIGNET BOOK

SIGNET
Published by New American Library, a division of
Penguin Group (USA) Inc., 375 Hudson Street,
New York, New York 10014, USA
Penguin Group (Canada), 90 Eglinton Avenue East, Suite 700, Toronto,
Ontario M4P 2Y3, Canada (a division of Pearson Penguin Canada Inc.)
Penguin Books Ltd., 80 Strand, London WC2R 0RL, England
Penguin Ireland, 25 St. Stephen's Green, Dublin 2,
Ireland (a division of Penguin Books Ltd.)
Penguin Group (Australia), 250 Camberwell Road, Camberwell, Victoria 3124,
Australia (a division of Pearson Australia Group Pty. Ltd.)
Penguin Books India Pvt. Ltd., 11 Community Centre, Panchsheel Park,
New Delhi - 110 017, India
Penguin Group (NZ), 67 Apollo Drive, Rosedale, Auckland 0632,
New Zealand (a division of Pearson New Zealand Ltd.)
Penguin Books (South Africa) (Pty.) Ltd., 24 Sturdee Avenue,
Rosebank, Johannesburg 2196, South Africa

Penguin Books Ltd., Registered Offices:
80 Strand, London WC2R 0RL, England

First published by Signet, an imprint of New American Library,
a division of Penguin Group (USA) Inc.

First Printing, August 2011
10  9  8  7  6  5  4  3  2  1

The first chapter of this book previously appeared in *Stagecoach Sidewinders*, the
three hundred fifty-seventh volume in this series.

Copyright © Penguin Group (USA) Inc., 2011
All rights reserved

 REGISTERED TRADEMARK—MARCA REGISTRADA

Printed in the United States of America

# The Trailsman

Beginnings . . . they bend the tree and they mark the man. Skye Fargo was born when he was eighteen. Terror was his midwife, vengeance his first cry. Killing spawned Skye Fargo, ruthless, cold-blooded murder. Out of the acrid smoke of gunpowder still hanging in the air, he rose, cried out a promise never forgotten.

The Trailsman they began to call him all across the West: searcher, scout, hunter, the man who could see where others only looked, his skills for hire but not his soul, the man who lived each day to the fullest, yet trailed each tomorrow. Skye Fargo, the Trailsman, the seeker who could take the wildness of a land and the wanting of a woman and make them his own.

*Santa Fe, New Mexico Territory, 1860—
where four murdering curs learn the hard way
what the word "friend" means to Skye Fargo.*

# 1

"C'mon out, old-timer!" shouted a thickset man hiding behind a mesquite tree. "We ain't desperadoes, just prospectors down on our luck! All we ask is a spot of grub."

"Prospectors! That's a hoot," retorted a tired and gravelly voice from inside the weather-beaten shack. "Ain't no color nowheres near here. And I've seed enough skunk-bit coyotes in my day. You aim to murder me, so let's get thrashing."

"Aww, hell, old roadster," Baylis Ulrick tried again. "This ain't Christian of you. My throat is parched and my backbone is scraping against my ribs."

"Happens you was just hungry men down on their luck," the old man shouted back, "you'd a just walked up and give me the hail. But I seen the four of you sneaking up on the place like warpath Comanches, clubs to hand. You've busted loose from a hoosegow someplace, and you mean to rob and kill me."

Ulrick was a big, heavy-jowled, flint-eyed man in homespun shirt and trousers and a rawhide vest. Like his companions hidden nearby in an erosion ditch, he was filthy and unshaven, his clothing sorely used. He gave the high sign to a hatchet-profiled man in the ditch. The man nodded and felt the sandy ground for a good rock.

"All right, we was locked up in Chimayo," Ulrick said, eyeing the shack's leather-hinged door. "We locked horns with some Mexers and got jugged for disturbing the peace."

"That's a neat trick seeing's how there ain't no sheriff *nor* jail in Chimayo. Not too many Mexers neither—'bout what you might expect in an Indian village."

The hatchet-profiled man had found a couple of rocks and

was trotting down the ditch, trying to get wide of the view from the shack's only window. The other two men twigged the game and headed in the opposite direction. The old salt was well armed and a good shot.

"Listen, Pop, nobody out west tells the truth. That don't make everybody killers. My hand to God, all we ask is a sup of water. We're all dry as a year-old cow chip. I give you my word we won't try a fox play."

"Your word don't mean spit. Now move on from here or my next shot won't be a warning."

Ulrick had a hair-trigger temper and it suddenly laid a red film over his vision. His breathing quickened until it whistled in his nostrils.

"If we're such hard cases," he shouted in a new tone of impatience, "how's come we ain't boosted that fine horseflesh in your corral? Ain't no window in the back of your shack. We coulda just rode out with 'em."

"Oh, you figger to do that, all right. But you need guns and food, too, and that means killing me. So let's just open the ball."

"Make you a deal, you old pus-gut. If you light out right now, we'll let you live. Otherwise, you'll die hard and I guarandamntee it."

"I got a better idea," the old man shot back. "Why'n'cha stick your dick in your ear and make a jug handle out of it?"

Immediately after this suggestion, his rifle spoke its piece. Baylis flinched hard when the slug raised a yellow plume of dust close to his exposed left foot. His eyes turned smoky with rage. Neither he nor the three men with him had a sulfur match between them, or they could have just burned the old rooster out.

Baylis glanced to his right and saw that Jed was in place. On his left, Hiram and Ray were almost set.

"All right, old man," he muttered, his tone heavy with menace. "It's time to fish or cut bait."

Despite his tough talk, Corey Webster tasted the corroded-pennies taste of fear.

Over his long life he had survived his share of scrapes. A man couldn't trap beaver with the likes of Caleb Greenwood

2

and Jim Bridger in the heyday of the Shining Times without sleeping on his weapons and shooting plumb every time. Corey had fought savages in the Stony Mountains before the U.S. Army even knew how to get there. And long before Skye Fargo became the famous Trailsman, Corey had helped to scrape the green off the kid's antlers.

But this today was dangerously different. In his mountain-man days the skirmishes were usually in the open, where a man could see around him and duck for cover. Now he was trapped in a clapboard box, and despite a bevy of good firearms he had foolishly run low on black powder and cartridges.

All these thoughts skittered around inside his head like frenzied rodents, but the old trapper was steady and determined, even fierce-eyed. Even his wooden leg had not banked his fires over the years.

He knew he was trapped between the sap and the bark. He could never manage to get horsed before this pack of mad dogs would bring him to ground. But without ammo, neither could he continue to hold them off from inside the shack.

Keeping his head sideways, Corey glanced out the window into the glaring sunshine. The big mouthpiece in the rawhide vest was still holed up behind the mesquite tree—he could see part of his left leg. But Corey knew he could no longer afford potshots. He was determined to plug at least one of these jackals before they sent him to glory.

His hands clutched a .44-caliber North & Savage rifle. He had traded some red fox furs for it in Santa Fe, realizing it would be a superb repeating weapon for scrapes just like this one. But Montezuma's revenge had given him a bad case of the trots and laid him up before he could stock up on loads.

He clicked the cylinder around—one shot left.

"Place is a goldang armory," he upbraided himself, "and all worthless. How many times did I tell Fargo a weapon without loads is like water without the wet?"

Corey had pulled a battered deal table in front of the door and piled his weapons on it. An old Kentucky over-and-under, a good gun, lay useless for lack of primer caps. Likewise with his four-barrel shotgun—each barrel had its own frizzen and pan, but he had no powder to pour into them.

"Where's them other three sonsabitches?" Corey wondered

aloud. He could no longer spot them peeking at the shack. Flanking the place, most likely, he realized.

"My offer is still good, old man," the mouthpiece shouted. "Light a shuck out of there now and you'll be gumming your supper tonight."

"Gum a cat's tail, you murderin' graveyard rat!"

A piece of foolscap on the table caught Corey's eye. He picked it up and read it.

*Corey, I hope the courier delivers this before I arrive in New Mexico Territory. The army is paying me rich man's wages to lead a mapmaking detail into the San-gre de Cristo Range. But if you're still alive, you tough old grizz, I plan to visit you first. The army can wait.*
*Skye*

"If I'm still alive," Corey repeated. "All hell's a-poppin', Skye. Ride in now, boy, and give this shit-eating trash a lead bath."

They were the last words ever spoken by Corey Webster. He glimpsed sudden movement to the left of the window and swung his rifle in that direction. An eyeblink later a tall, skinny man jumped in from the right, a classic diversion. His right arm was already cocked and released a fist-size rock at Corey almost point-blank. Force like a mule kick made the old man stagger back as an orange starburst exploded inside his skull.

He folded like an empty sack, the rifle dropping to the rammed-earth floor beside him. A cheer erupted from without.

"Nice work, Jed," Baylis Ulrick called out as he ran toward the shack. "You brained the old bastard good."

The four men struggled for a moment to open the blocked door, then crowded into the one-room shack. Hiram Steele, a small, hard-knit man with furtive eyes and a pockmarked face, knelt beside the old-timer.

"Christ on a crutch!" he exclaimed. "Half his forehead is crushed in like an eggshell, but the old goat is still breathing!"

Ulrick's eyes flicked toward the bowie knife on the table. "Not for long he ain't, chappies."

Hearing this, the other three men exchanged silent glances.

Ulrick, with his hard-hitting fists and take-charge manner, was a natural-born leader of desperate men. But before he took to the owlhoot trail he had been trained as a butcher in Chicago. As they had recently learned, he had not completely left his old trade behind.

"Wood ticks in my Johnny!" exclaimed a man with green-rimmed teeth and gums the color of raw liver. Ray Nearhood pointed to a shelf made of crossed sticks. It held modest but welcome provisions: a cheesecloth sack filled with jerked beef, cans of coffee and sugar, a sack of cornmeal.

"And glom the weapons the old cheese dick had," Jed Longstreet marveled, picking up the heavy but dangerous-looking flintlock shotgun. "This thing's a relic but, by hell, it's got four barrels! You rotate 'em by hand."

He did so, and all four men were impressed at the sharp, precise clicks as each barrel snapped into place. The vintage weapon was in mint condition.

"I seen them hand cannons in the Mexican War," Baylis explained. "A man could toss a biscuit farther than that piece shoots. But close up, one shot will strip the clothes off three men standing shoulder to shoulder. It's heavy, but we'll pack it along. Might come in handy."

Hiram Steele picked up the North & Savage. "Thissen's old, too, but it's a repeater. The trigger guard is combined with the lever, see? When you move it you revolve the cylinder and cock the hammer."

"It's big-bore so we'll take it," Ulrick decided. "Piss on that Kentucky rifle. We'll get more guns someplace. See any ammo?"

As the men looked around, Longstreet spotted the letter under the table. He swooped down to pick it up. "Any of you boys know how to read?"

Ulrick snatched it from his hand and read it aloud.

"Katy Christ!" Nearhood erupted when Baylis read the signature. "This old fartsack was chums with the Trailsman?"

"Who's this Trailsman?" demanded Hiram, busy tossing the provisions into a gunnysack.

"Where you been grazing?" Nearhood replied. "They say he's the toughest hombre ever born of woman."

"The Trailsman," Longstreet chimed in. "Well, carry me

out. Carry me out with tongs! They claim he can track an ant across rocks."

"That's bad news," Ulrick sneered, "for ants."

"Ray ain't birding," Longstreet assured him. "I hear Fargo is six sorts of trouble. And if he's coming to visit this old geezer, they must be chummy. Baylis, maybe you oughtn't to . . . you know, carve him up like you done them guards in the Manzanos."

Ulrick's big, bluff features twisted into a mask of contempt. "Shit, listen to the ladies' sewing circle! You boys believe too much barroom josh. Anyhow, you know how it is with travel time out here. Fargo could be a month off still. Ain't no witnesses saw us, so how will the big bad Trailsman even know who to trail?"

"That rings right," Nearhood agreed. "'Sides, Apaches, Kiowa, and Comanches raid in these parts. The way Baylis sets to work, it looks like wild Indians done it."

Ulrick nodded. "That's the gait. You boys round up whatever tack you can and get them horses ready to raise dust."

He picked up the bowie knife from the table and tested its edge with a finger. "Not bad. I wish I had me a boning knife and a cleaver, too, but this is all right for rough-gutting."

"I don't like it," Longstreet objected again. "It's bad enough that Fargo will find his old pal cold as a wagon wheel. Why poke fire with a sword by butchering him out?"

Baylis squatted, stiff kneecaps popping. "Finding his chum with a crushed skull will surely raise Fargo's ire. But finding him with his entrails stacked on his chest just might scare the fight out of him."

"Maybe," Longstreet said as he went out the door. "But that ain't what I hear."

# 2

The lazy clip-clop of shod hooves barely disturbed the peaceful, sun-shot day. The two riders, one clad in fringed buckskins, the other in military blue, held their mounts to a long trot. A yellow cloud of dust boiled up behind the riders, powdering the scant growth along both sides of the Old Pueblo Trail.

"Mr. Fargo," said Second Lieutenant Wade McKenna, his voice breaking the lazy stillness, "you aren't too keen on us Academy graduates, are you?"

Fargo lifted one hand from the reins to shove his broad-brimmed plainsman's hat higher on his brow. "Mr. McKenna, that's a libel on me. But seeing as how you're still frying size, I'll forgive it."

His head swiveled right to study the young officer from piercing, lake blue eyes. He saw a rangy, clean-cut towhead, a young sprout of twenty or so. He was fresh off the benches at West Point with his head full of "field tactics" from the days of Napoleon and set-piece battles on open fields. But since riding out from Medicine Lodge Creek back in the Indian Territory, Fargo had grown to like him.

"Just because the wood is green," he added, "doesn't mean it's not sturdy and full of sap. West Point men are a credit to their dams. It's West Point that's the problem. They do a fine job of teaching you all the wrong things—wrong, anyhow, for the American West."

"I agree," McKenna said eagerly. "Just in the nine days I've been riding with you, I've got a new education."

Fargo's strong white teeth flashed through his cropped beard. "No, you've got *started* on it. On the frontier the

7

lessons never stop. Especially out here in the barren land of Coronado."

"Yes, sir. I can't tell you how proud I am that you let me ride with you to my new post. Why, you've been written up—"

Fargo raised one hand. "Turn off the tap, Lieutenant. Save all that starry-eyed bosh for when you meet the Queen of England. And, Christ sakes, would you bottle all that 'sir' business? Hell, I'm wearing bloody buckskins. Just call me Mr. Fargo or just plain Fargo."

"All right, Just Plain Fargo."

Both men laughed.

"Now you're getting salty," Fargo approved. "But remember, we ain't swapping spit."

Fargo had recently been summoned from the Indian Territory, where he'd been serving as a contract scout, for a special assignment to guide U.S. Army cartographers mapping the Sangre de Cristo Range of the southern Rockies. Wade McKenna, receiving his transfer orders to the Third Cavalry Regiment at the same time, had been delayed by a lack of transportation. Not too keen on the idea, Fargo had nonetheless agreed to take the officer with him.

They topped a high ridge offering an excellent view, and Fargo reined in his black-and-white stallion. Although white-capped mountains surrounded them on the distant horizons, up close the terrain was mostly gentle scrub hills dotted with creosote and cholla. Long ago they had left the level ranges pockmarked by prairie dog towns. Fargo, however, did not study it with a painter's eye—he scrutinized all of it with the relaxed but vigilant eye of a wary frontiersman.

"Looks pretty—and peaceful," McKenna said, lifting his bull's-eye canteen for a drink. Fargo stifled a grin when the kid hastily put his canteen away without taking a sip. He had just remembered one of Professor Fargo's lessons: Never drink under a hot sun.

"It always looks peaceful until it isn't," Fargo replied. "See how this country is almost all greens and browns? That tends to mask color and shapes. Keep your eyes focused for distance and look for movement, not shapes."

"Wish I had a notebook," Wade muttered.

Fargo snorted and shook his head. "You have. It's mounted on your shoulders. Just harken and heed."

They gigged their mounts forward, bearing due south.

"Think we'll reach Santa Fe today?" the young officer asked.

"We might if we took the Raton Pass. But it's strewn with rocks and prone to laming horses. It's a little longer, but we're going to take the Cimarron Cutoff."

"Raton," McKenna repeated. "Raton . . . isn't that Spanish for rat?"

Fargo nodded. "You palaver the language?"

"Some. You?"

"Enough to bargain with the prettier whores."

The kid looked skeptical. "Back at Fort Monroe, it's said you don't, uhh . . . consort with whores."

"There's another slander. I 'uhh . . . consort' with them, all right. I just don't uhh . . . *pay* them. There's always volunteers even among mercenaries. Now, you gotta admit—*that's* a bargain."

"Santa Fe," the kid said wonderingly. "The City of the Holy Faith. What's it like, sir—I mean, Mr. Fargo?"

"You'll find out soon enough. It's like no other city in America. I'll tell you that much. There is a lot of holy faith there, and a lot of holy hell, too."

"I've read it's the oldest city in the country. Hundreds of years old."

Fargo backhanded sweat off his forehead, eyes in slow, constant motion. "Sure. Goes back to the Spanish dons and the Pueblo Indians before them. Now the Anglos own it. That's what you have to remember as a soldier because the bloodletting goes way back, too. There's old scores still being settled."

McKenna's voice turned solemn. "Yeah. Despite all the engineering and mathematics classes at the Point, they did manage to teach us about the Apaches. And I hear they raid in this area."

"They do, but mostly they stick to the mountains and pick on the Pueblos. Those are peaceful, Christianized tribes and they've learned not to resist invaders. But some of the Mexicans still lay claim to this place—hell, it's barely ten years

**9**

ago we took it from 'em. And a place with as much wealth as moves through here on its way to the King's Highway into deep Mexico draws plenty of white hard cases, too."

"This Chimayo where your friend Corey Webster lives . . . what's it like?"

At mention of his old friend and trail mentor, Fargo's face, nut brown from years in the saddle, creased in a fond grin.

"Chimayo? Hell, it's just a flyspeck fifty miles northwest of Santa Fe. Indian village clumped around an adobe church. But Corey lives outside of the place. He's a bunch-quitter from way back. Once a place peoples up, he gets fiddle-footed. Some old mountain men live in the cities now and sell their tales. Not that stubborn old goat."

"One of the fellows back at the sutler's store at Fort Monroe," the shavetail prodded, "said he saved your life."

"Now *that* was no libel. But saving a man's life is one thing—paying a hell of a sacrifice to do it is another. He didn't just save my life, Lieutenant—he bought me a future and paid a dear price."

McKenna was clearly primed to learn more. But Fargo rarely spoke of things that were truly important to him, things he couldn't shape into words. Besides, these past couple of days, every time he thought about broaching a keg in friendship with Corey, a vague foreboding made his scalp tingle. After all, he hadn't heard from his old comrade in almost two years—maybe the old salt had given up the ghost.

They rode on for another two miles in silence, seeing nothing more ominous than a small black bear that briefly unsettled the horses. They rounded the shoulder of a hill covered with jack pines and Fargo drew back on the reins again.

"There's a little seep spring just ahead," he told the soldier. "Inside that copse on the right. Wait here while I take a squint."

"You expecting trouble?" McKenna asked, his voice tight with excitement.

"Best to look before you wade in," Fargo said matter-of-factly. He threw the reins forward to hold the Ovaro in place, then swung down. He knocked the leather riding thong off the hammer of his Colt as he walked cautiously forward.

"It's all right," he called out a few moments later. "Lead the horses in."

"Damnation, Mr. Fargo," the lieutenant marveled as he entered the shady copse. "You travel the entire West—how can you remember all these places?"

"It's a wonder," Fargo replied slyly. "I mean, without a notebook."

The towhead flushed to the roots of his hair. "I deserve that."

The spot was cool and restful after the dust and sun of the trail. Woodpeckers kept up a steady rat-a-tat-tat from the trees overhead.

"Fresh spring water," McKenna said, leading his big cavalry sorrel toward the spring.

"As you were, you young fool," Fargo barked behind him.

McKenna turned around, his face perplexed. "What's wrong? I'm just going to water my horse. They've been at an easy pace and need no cooling down first."

"Before we drink and dip our heads into that water first?"

"But—I mean, you're always harping on how the horses come first."

Fargo shook his head. "Jesus God Almighty. Wade, haven't you ever noticed that a horse pisses while it drinks? Pisses a *long* time?"

The kid stood there a full minute, looking foolish and stupid. "Yeah, you're right. At the Academy we learn more about algebra than we do horses."

"Imagine that," Fargo said, a sarcastic edge to his voice. "Suffer the little children . . ."

The men flopped onto their bellies, drank deeply, plunged their heads into the bracing water, and then filled their canteens. While the horses tanked up, McKenna admired the Ovaro.

"That stallion of yours is some pumpkins, Mr. Fargo. They say he can outrun a Comanche warhorse."

"Oh, I reckon he's a mite better than a plow nag," Fargo allowed.

Perhaps understanding this, the Ovaro's tail suddenly lashed out and swiped Fargo in the face.

"Not too sensitive, either," the Trailsman added.

"Comet here," McKenna said, watching his sorrel now, "is good horseflesh. Seventeen hands high and wrapped in hard muscle."

"A cavalry horse is all right," Fargo agreed, "long as you don't ask too much of it. Big, strong, and smart. But they're coddled in garrison. The policy of graining them every day spoils them for grass on long campaigns. Hell, this pinto of mine will eat tree bark in a pinch."

Fargo slid his Colt from the holster and palmed the wheel to check his loads. Both men then pulled their horses back from the water so they wouldn't be loggy on the trail. They cinched the girth and stepped up into leather, turning their horses back toward the Old Pueblo Road.

"This next stretch is favored by bandits," Fargo warned his companion. "I was dry-gulched near here once. Keep your eyes skinned."

"What happened?" the kid demanded eagerly.

"Well, they wanted my rifle. All they got were a dozen or so of the bullets—minus the shell casings."

McKenna studied the lever-action, brass-framed Henry protruding from Fargo's saddle scabbard. "Sixteen shots . . . they say you can load it on Sunday and fire it all week."

"It ain't perfect. I always pack along an extra magazine on account the thin metal of the tube bends too easy. But it's the first reliable repeating rifle invented with the frontiersman in mind."

"You would know. But the barrel is so goldang long. How can you skirmish in close places like thick woods?"

"It can get rough," Fargo admitted. "Plenty of times I have to leave it in the scabbard. But mostly I'm in open country and that's when that long barrel pays its freight. Now that little Spencer of yours"—Fargo nodded toward the cavalry-issue 7-shot carbine in Wade's saddle boot—"is a good skirmish gun in short battles. It's accurate out to three hundred yards, the .56 slug packs a wallop, and it's easy to load from the saddle by just shoving rounds through that trap in the butt plate. But having so little barrel, it heats up too quick."

"We were warned about that at the Academy," McKenna said. "The slugs are copper-jacketed, and when the gun heats they get soft and can stick in the ejector."

Fargo nodded. "Someday it's going to happen when Soldier Blue is surrounded by warpath Indians. You fellows would be better off with Henrys."

"Never," McKenna boasted. "Sure, Indians don't lack for courage, and now and then they kill soldiers out on small details. But they lack tactics. West Point men will outwit them every time in large battles."

"It's a brevet or a coffin for you, eh?" Fargo said, not really too interested. He had spotted four riders in the sandy valley below the trail, bearing in the direction of Santa Fe from the north. He pulled the army binoculars from one of his saddle pockets.

"Trouble?" the shavetail said, his tone hopeful.

"For somebody," Fargo replied. "The sun's at a bad angle, I can't make out their faces or the markings of their horses. But those are definitely four hard cases on the prod."

"How can you tell so quick?" Wade pulled his own glasses out and looked below them.

"For one thing, only one of them has a saddle. White men don't ride bareback unless they're in a circus."

"Yeah, only the one in front has one."

"Those are Indian scrubs they're riding," Fargo added. "See how their tails are almost brushing the ground? And their manes are so long they have to keep tossing their heads to clear their vision."

Wade snorted. "The ones without saddles don't know how to ride bareback—they're really pounding their testicles."

The intense glare kept Fargo from making out any weapons, too. But he saw the lumpy gunnysack tied to one man's belt. Some kind of loot, likely.

"Should we ride down and challenge them?" Wade asked. "We can't arrest them, but maybe we can report them to the sheriff in Santa Fe."

Fargo shook his head. "With me it's live and let live. All four of those jaspers are prob'ly so low they could walk under a snake's belly on stilts. Murderers, likely, way they're skulking through rough terrain instead of using the trail. But nobody made *me* ten inches taller than God, nor you either. This is an organized territory, not the uncharted frontier. Let the law dogs handle this bunch."

Fargo put away his spyglasses and gazed up into an endless summer sky of seamless blue. He gigged the Ovaro forward. "C'mon, Lieutenant, we're burning daylight. I've got a good campsite in mind, about two hours ahead. We don't want to be on this trail after sundown."

They chucked their mounts up to a long trot. But despite his dismissive words just now, Fargo couldn't push those four hard cases from his thoughts.

*Bearing in the direction of Santa Fe from the north.*

*Murderers, likely.*

*He didn't just save my life, Lieutenant—he bought me a future and paid a dear price.*

# 3

Hell of a thing, thought rancher Judd Sloan. A man celebrates the life of a saint by going into town and getting drunk. These Mexicans were a strange lot.

He rode slowly along the western border of his New Mexico spread, checking for breaks in the split-rail fence. In the waning light of a hot, windless day he watched clumps of longhorn cattle taking off the grass. Longhorns were a mean, half-wild lot and he avoided any sudden movements—they had been dubbed ladinos by the two Mexican vaqueros who worked for him, "sly ones." A few in the herd were even potential man-killers.

Both of his ranch hands, who suddenly became zealously religious for saint festivals, were in Santa Fe right now and would ride home late tonight stinking of cactus liquor. But both would be back in the saddle by sunup and put in a good day's work for a meager day's pay. Yessir, a strange lot.

This was a small spread, only three hundred head, and would yield tough, stringy meat. But a head of beef currently sold for forty dollars in the capital, and if he drove only a third of his herd to market, it would sell for the incredible price of four thousand dollars. Then he could hire more men, increase the herd next year, and soon enough he could move his family into a mansion on Santa Fe's prestigious College Street.

"You're mighty damn lucky, Sloan," he reminded himself.

Lucky as all hell to even have this place and a beautiful wife and daughter to share it with. There was plenty of talk lately about a homestead act coming to the western territories, but he'd gotten a head start on that. Martha had a Spanish ancestor somewhere in her family tree, and by the land-grant laws still legal in New Mexico, this place had been left to her by some Spanish viceroy they'd never even met.

It was well worth giving up a stump farm in Michigan to come out here even if the workdays did stretch from can to can't. Soon enough—

A man's groan of pain reached him from a little pine thicket on his left. Sloan automatically pulled the Volcanic lever-action repeating rifle from its scabbard and nudged his big claybank in that direction.

"Who's in there?" he called out, squinting to see better in the shadowy interior of the thicket.

Another groan was the only reply.

Sloan swung down and wrapped the reins around a nearby tree. He moved cautiously into the thicket. Almost immediately he spotted a big man in a rawhide vest sprawled face-down on the ground.

"Mister! Hey, mister! Can you hear me?"

No reply except another groan that sounded weaker. Sloan moved closer, grounded his rifle, and knelt beside the stranger. Gingerly, he began to roll him over.

As he did, a sudden clicking sound from thousands of insects filled the thicket. Sloan recognized it—the sound of wood-boring beetles. What were they called? There were old legends about them he recalled from his childhood.

Then he remembered: deathwatch beetles. Said to suddenly make their sound when someone was about to . . .

Sloan's scalp tightened and his face broke out in sweat. Abruptly, he sprang back up and raced toward his horse.

"Shit, Baylis!" called out a voice from farther back inside the thicket. "The bastard's getting away!"

Sloan freed his reins and vaulted into the saddle. He had spun the claybank halfway around when Ulrick launched the bowie. A scarlet rope of blood erupted from Judd Sloan's neck. He dropped his rifle and slumped in the saddle, choking on his own blood, then slipped from the horse, one foot caught in the stirrup. The claybank panicked and bolted off with Sloan's body bumping and leaping over the uneven ground.

"Damn my eyes!" Jed Longstreet told his leader. "I knew

you rated aces high as a butcher, but you never told us you could *throw* a knife, too."

"I can't. It was a lucky throw."

"Not too lucky for that damn cow nurse," Hiram Steele said.

Baylis climbed to his feet, brushing the dirt off his trousers. He picked up the Volcanic repeater. "That's what happens to good Samaritans in New Mexico Territory. C'mon, boys. Let's get up to the house before the horse returns dragging that body."

They had looked the place over good before hiding their horses in a nearby woods. The spread was located in a fertile piece of bottomland a few hours north of Santa Fe—a low, split-log house with a stone well out back and a long stone watering trough in front of the modest barn.

"He must have hired hands," Ulrick remarked as they moved out of the thicket and toward the house. "But I don't see anybody."

Halfway to the house they encountered a small, window-less shed constructed over a spring to keep food cold.

"Fresh provisions, boys," Ulrick said. "*Now* we'll stoke our bellies. Anybody see that damn claybank?"

Longstreet's hatchet profile turned toward the north. "It's way to hellangone. We got time before it comes back. That old man's jerky is laying heavy on my chest. Let's check the vittles."

The men crowded inside. One board shelf held jars of pickles and preserves.

"Fresh buttermilk!" Ray Nearhood exclaimed, flashing his green teeth as he uncovered a crockery jug.

"Nobody hogs it," Ulrick ordered. "We go equal shares."

"Son of a damn bitch, here's a whole ham!" Hiram Steele pitched in, uncovering a huge platter.

Each man tore off a hunk and ate ravenously, washing the meat down with buttermilk. Ulrick finished first and wiped his greasy hands on his pants, watching the ranch house through the front door of the little springhouse. He took out the makings he'd found at the old man's shack and built himself a cigarette while the others finished eating.

"Still no sign of hired hands," he mused aloud. "Don't make sense. One man couldn't work all this cattle."

"Maybe he's got sons," Longstreet suggested around a mouthful of food.

"Better yet, daughters," Hiram Steele reminded the others. "I ain't had no cunny in a long time."

"Join the club," Longstreet told him. "My point, chucklehead, is that sons will mean guns."

Ulrick nodded. "That's what I'm thinking, too. And in this territory they're likely to have their weapons to hand."

"Why, sure," said Steele from a deadpan face. "There's riffraff all over."

Ulrick was the only one who didn't laugh. "Stow it, Hiram, and for now get the foofaraw outta your mind until it's safe. We have to be careful. This rifle has a full magazine, but there's only one load in that North & Savage, and the bowie is still in that corpse. We have to do this careful-like or all four of us could be picking lead out of our livers."

He flipped his butt away in a wide arc. "All right. Let's go pay our respects up at the house."

"Pa must have found another break in the fence," Kristen Sloan remarked to her mother, watching the last sunlight fade in copper reflections on the windowpanes. "Those longhorns are certainly rambunctious animals."

"They are that," Martha agreed. "But that raggedy herd is going to help us put by against the future, young woman."

"I know," the pretty, chestnut-haired girl said petulantly. "Seems like that's all we ever talk about—the future. And when it finally comes, I'll be an old maid."

Martha, busy turning up the wick of a coal-oil lamp to light it, laughed. "Laws! Just turned eighteen and she thinks life has passed her by. You'll see, honey. Your hardworking pa will have us in Santa Fe and wearing French gowns long before you lose your looks."

Kristen, who had been out riding, wore a split buckskin skirt and a leather jerkin. Her hair tumbled loose over her shoulders.

"You're right on that last point, Ma," she relented. "You sure haven't lost your looks yet. Pa's right: pretty as four aces."

"Bosh!" Martha said, obviously pleased. She set the glass chimney on the lamp and soft yellow light pushed the shadows back into the corners of the parlor, revealing a fieldstone fireplace, bearskin rugs scattered across a plank floor, and a cherry spinet against the back wall.

"Where in tarnation could that man be?" Martha wondered. "I s'pose with Juan and Paco off in town he's trying to do three men's work."

Both women recognized a slight creaking noise from the back of the house—the latchstring being lifted and the door pushed open.

"Here he comes," Martha said. "He'll be hungry as a spring bear. Honey, run out to the springhouse and get the ham, would you? Bring the buttermilk, too. It settles his stomach."

"His stomach has been settled," a strange voice said from the hallway. "Settled for good."

One after another, four of the filthiest desperadoes either woman had ever seen or imagined stepped into the parlor. The one in the rawhide vest was huge and barrel-chested, the one following him tall and skinny and hatchet-faced. The third one was small and glanced around like a nervous rat. The last one in leered like a half-wit, his teeth and gums horrid to behold.

"That's my husband's rifle," accused Martha, staring at the Volcanic now aimed at her lights.

"Well, see," Ulrick replied, enjoying this immensely, "he sorta got scared and left it behind."

"You trash," Martha said.

"Oh, trash ain't got nothing on us, dumplin'," Ulrick assured her. "Matter fact, I just murdered your man. No more slap 'n' tickle for you two."

"You oughter see him," Longstreet chimed in, keeping the North & Savage trained on the girl. "Got his foot hung up in a stirrup after Baylis here buried a bowie in his throat. He's out there bouncing around like a big old rag doll."

Kristen, her face chalk white, began to quietly sob. For a few moments Martha felt like she was trying to stand up in a dugout on a raging river. But the worst, she realized, was yet to come and she had to be ready.

Green teeth sidled up beside Kristen. "No need to have a

**19**

conniption, sugar britches. All of us is here to console you in your hour of loss."

He reached out to grab a breast, but she sidestepped him.

"Wiggle all you want to," he taunted her. "All four of us is going to plant our carrots in both of you."

"There's got to be more men around here than just your husband," Ulrick said. "Where are they?"

Martha tried to speak, but her mouth wouldn't respond to her will.

"Ray," Ulrick said.

Green teeth backhanded Kristen so hard that she swayed on her feet.

"Stop it!" Martha pleaded. "I'll tell you anything you want to know."

Ulrick's lips curled into a sneer. "Damn straight you will, bitch. Now where's the men?"

"There's no boys in the family, it's just the . . . the three of us. There's two Mexican hired hands. They sleep in the barn. But they're off at the saint's festival in Santa Fe and won't be back until late tonight."

All four men exchanged glances, grinning.

"Four foxes in the henhouse," Longstreet said. "My, oh my."

"Hell, we got time to start with a quick poke," Ulrick decided. "Hiram, strip that filly buck. Ray, you strip Mama. I'm gunna screw each one of 'em while the other watches."

Martha's heart leaped into her throat and a shudder moved up her spine like a cold finger. She had known this moment was coming from the time she first laid eyes on these hell-spawned monsters. Now, for Kristen's sake, she had to be strong.

One hand had been knotted in the pocket of her calico housedress. Before the rat-eyed man with the pocked face could touch Kristen, Martha pulled the two-shot .50 caliber hideout gun from her pocket. But she had already done the horrific math: Two shots, and four men, meant that at least two would still be alive after her bullets were spent. And that assumed she could even aim accurately with her arm trembling like this.

"Honey, I love you!" she cried as she brought the short muzzles up to Kristen's head and fired. A bloody spray of blood, brain matter, and bone fragments erupted all over Steele.

Ulrick and Longstreet were too surprised to react before Martha raised the gun to her own temple and fired. She folded to the floor dead, landing atop her daughter.

"Well, cuss my coup!" Ray Nearhood exclaimed. "There goes our pussy and me already hard!"

"Hell, poon is out there for the taking," Ulrick said. "We'll get our packages wrapped before too long. Never mind for now. Hiram!"

"Yo!"

"Sack this place. Keep an eye peeled for weapons and men's clothes and boots. There's a lean-to bedroom off the rear of the house. Search it good for money. There's no banks around here and ranchers don't trust 'em anyhow. Ray, get away from them damn bodies!"

Nearhood had been about to pull the daughter's buckskin skirt off. He stood up, scowling. "I just want to take a look at her, is all."

"Never mind. Get out to the barn and gather up all the saddles and tack. There's about a dozen horses in the corral. Pick ones with the most common markings—lineback duns are common down here. Jed"—he turned to Longstreet—"get out by the road and stand watch in them cottonwoods. You see anybody headed this way, give the hail."

Longstreet nodded. A grin twitched his lips apart. "What are you gonna be doing, boss? Poking them dead gals before they go cold?"

Ulrick's breathing quickened as he studied the fine set of knives he could see in a case on the kitchen wall. "Speak the truth and shame the devil, Jed. Definitely gonna be some poking."

# 4

When the sun was a dull red coin balanced on the western horizon, Fargo kept his eyes open for a good campsite. He soon found one in a sheltered copse about fifty feet off the trail. It was in the lee of a steep slope with a small brook splashing down.

"This is what you want in a campsite," Fargo told his companion as they led their horses in. "Water, shelter from wind so you can make a fire, and few approaches for your enemy. And with the moon in full phase, plenty of trees to darken the place."

"I'm glad to hear you mention a fire," McKenna said. "I'm hungry as a field hand. My belly is starting to rebel at all this hardtack and jerked beef."

"I'll fry up some salt pork," Fargo said as he stripped the leather from his mount. "And bake some corn dodgers in the ashes. You can boil the coffee."

Both men wiped their horses down with old gunnysacks and quickly ran a currycomb over them. Since this water was moving swiftly, they let the horses drink first, then placed them on short tethers.

"The only thing this place lacks is grass," Fargo said, "so we'll grain 'em tonight. They could use it anyway. They've had damn little time to graze."

Fargo gathered wood and took a handful of crumbled bark from one of his saddle pockets to start a fire.

"Those four riders we saw earlier," McKenna said, busy with Fargo's blue enameled coffeepot. "Couldn't they just be prospectors or something down on their luck? Maybe Indians jumped them and stole their gear."

"Most of the Indians that belong to this territory," Fargo said, "are generally law-abiding. They haven't raised hell since the Pueblo Indian Revolt a couple centuries ago. Now, the Apaches do range here, and that bunch would never just steal from white-eyes—they'd kill them. Prob'ly stone them to death—an Apache won't waste a bullet on a Mexican or a white."

"Maybe claim jumpers left that bunch so desperate," McKenna mused.

"What? Stole their horses and left them four Indian scrubs? They showed all the signs of criminals on the prod."

"You would know," Wade conceded, pouring out the coffee. "Is that grub ready?"

"Hell, dig in, Lieutenant. Just because you're an officer don't make me your mess man."

The men ate their salt pork while Fargo formed little balls from cornmeal and water and tossed them into the hot ashes to cook. They tasted good dunked into the strong coffee, but Wade's question about the four men had Fargo worrying again. Not only were they riding from the direction of Chimayo, but on Indian scrubs—and Corey Webster was known to trade and sell such mounts.

But Fargo shook off his pensive mood like a dog shaking off water. Even if those horses had belonged to Corey, that didn't mean they weren't legally traded or sold. Corey was gruff, but not heartless—it wouldn't be unlike him to practically give those mounts to strangers who were down and out. And anybody trying to intimidate him—even four men— would be up against one of the toughest grizzlies on the American frontier. One who kept plenty of weapons to hand.

Both men poured a shot of whiskey into their second cup of coffee and enjoyed it with thin black Mexican cigars Fargo pulled from his shirt pocket.

"Nothing like a good cigar," the kid declared, eyes watering from the powerful black shag tobacco.

"If you like it that much," Fargo said, hiding a grin behind his hand, "I have more."

"No, no," the shavetail said quickly, "fine tobacco should be savored like fine wine."

When it was time to turn in, Fargo loaned the officer his Arkansas toothpick and showed him how to soften the rocky ground under his bedroll.

"Before you crawl in," Fargo said, "might be a good idea to loop your rope in a circle around your bedroll. Rattlesnakes won't crawl over a rope."

"I read that's just an old wives' tale."

"Maybe so, but old wives know a lot. I been sleeping on the ground most of my life, and I haven't had a rattlesnake crawl into my bedroll yet."

"But I'll bet you've been snakebit plenty, huh?"

"More times than I care to remember," Fargo said. "One rattlesnake bite won't generally kill a healthy adult, but it will lay you out sick and miserable for two days. Hurts like the dickens, too. They sink those fangs in deep."

Fargo checked on the horses and kicked dirt over the fire before rolling up in his blanket. He was bone-weary from the long ride of the past nine days, and the steady chuckle of the mountain brook quickly began to lull him. Somewhere far off a panther screamed, but it was quickly absorbed in the steady drone of cicadas.

Instead of falling asleep, however, Fargo suddenly sat up. "Wade, you asleep?"

"Huh? What? What is it, Mr. Fargo?"

The young officer had indeed been fast asleep, but in the buttery moonlight Fargo watched him shoot up to his knees, his .44 Colt service revolver in his hand.

"Hop your horse," Fargo told him, his tone brooking no defiance. "We're riding to Chimayo."

McKenna, conditioned to accept imperious commands without question, quietly rigged his sorrel in the generous moon wash.

"I know what you're thinking," Fargo told him as he slipped on the bridle and the Ovaro easily took the bit. "Why are we riding after dark after all the harping I've done about the dangers of laming a horse?"

"There's that," the kid admitted. "But mostly I'm wondering what just suddenly got into you to change our plan about going to Santa Fe first."

"Don't worry about your orders. You've got twelve days to make the trip and we're well under that."

"Hang the orders. It's just . . . your mind was at peace when you turned in. Did you have a dream or something?"

"I didn't even fall asleep."

Fargo hated to stonewall the kid, but some things eluded language. What had changed Fargo's mind was something he called a "God fear"—a warning instinct as real as a hand on the back of his neck.

"Just call it a frontiersman's hunch," he finally said. "Far as riding after dark—there'll be danger, all right, for us and the horses. But there's a full moon and a cloudless sky."

"Will we stick to the Old Pueblo Road?"

"No. We're heading north through the mountains. But we can pick up a good trail just ahead. The real danger is from bandits. With luck, we can reach Corey's place along about sunup."

Despite his urgency, Fargo carefully inspected his saddle, cinches, latigos, and stirrups. He made sure his Colt and his spare cylinder were both loaded with six slugs.

"Ready?" he asked, forking leather and wheeling the Ovaro around toward the road.

"Up and on the line, sir!" the game young soldier called out, falling in behind him.

An hour's uneventful ride, holding a steady lope, brought them to the trail Fargo had mentioned, an ancient Indian game trace later widened by fur trappers and army supply wagons. Now it was called the Chimayo-Santa Fe Road and saw little traffic—of a legal nature.

At first, winding along the lower slopes of the Sangre de Cristo Range, it was easy riding. Fargo began to feel foolish. He had dragged both of them, not to mention two tired horses, out of a badly needed sleep to chase after *odjib*, an Indian word for "a thing of smoke."

The Ovaro whickered and pricked his ears forward, a trouble sign Fargo never ignored.

"We got a dustup coming," he warned McKenna. "Break out your Spencer and jack a round into the chamber."

They rounded a bend in the trail and Fargo saw shadowy forms blocking the trail.

"Road agents," he said tersely. "They plan to rob us and steal our horses. I count at least six. Listen, kid, they expect us to either stop when they order us to or to turn around and hightail it. So what would a good West Point officer do?"

"The unexpected," McKenna answered without hesitation. "Surprise, mystify, and confuse your enemies."

"My credo, too. So wait for my command. When you hear me gig my horse to a gallop, you do the same. When I open up with my Henry, you start cracking caps with the carbine. You've got a big, strong gelding, and my stallion could ride through a stone wall. We hit them full bore behind a wall of lead."

"Yes, sir," the kid replied. His voice was nervous but he also sounded game.

"One more thing. This trail is narrow with trees tight against us on both sides. Normally I'd tell you to shoot for the horses, not the men—easier targets at night. But dead horses could block us long enough for these maggots to shoot us. So whatever you do, shoot above the saddles. Once we're past them, I'll drop a bead on the horses."

The shadows ahead were looming closer. McKenna copied Fargo when he flattened himself against his horse's neck to make a smaller target.

"Hee-*yah!*" Fargo shouted, thumping the Ovaro with his heels.

The stalwart pinto was eager to run after days of trotting. He laid back his ears and surged forward with impressive speed and power, the cavalry sorrel making a good showing beside him.

"Put at 'em!" Fargo ordered, firing his Henry over the Ovaro's head.

McKenna's Spencer cracked, muzzle spitting orange flame, and the shooting fray was on. The two riders laid down a withering field of fire, and Fargo watched one man slump in his saddle. The bandits returned fire, and Fargo could hear their bullets zwipping through the tree branches crowding him on both sides.

Fargo held on tight with both legs to free his hands for working the Henry's lever. Rather than waste time reloading the Spencer, McKenna broke out his sidearm. At least two men still blocked the trail but Fargo refused to slacken the pace.

"Keep up the strut, kid!" he shouted. "Nothing stops us!"

Bullets snapped past close to Fargo's ears, and one twitched his left leg when it hit the stirrup. But Fargo thundered forward like the Apocalypse, hot lead heralding his arrival. There was a sharp cry of *"Maldito"* when a second man twisted in his saddle.

"They aren't moving!" McKenna said urgently when the two galloping horsebackers were almost on their enemy.

"They'll move," Fargo assured him, "or these warhorses of ours will move them."

His prediction rang true. At the last possible moment the highwaymen gave up their bluff and nudged their mounts aside. Fargo and McKenna streaked past them, bullets nipping at their heels.

Fargo had no intention of making it easy for these scrotes to dog them from behind. Never missing a beat, he pulled his feet from the stirrups and tucked his Henry tight under one arm. Then he pushed up from the saddle on both hands and revolved around until he was facing backward, a trick he had learned from the Northern Cheyennes.

Braced against the cantle, he sent lead whistling toward the pursuing cutthroats. The 16-shot Henry still held half its loads, and this time he aimed for horses. He heard at least two mounts crash into the thick growth, and then all sounds of pursuit ceased.

"Moses on the mountain!" McKenna exclaimed, watching the Trailsman right himself in the saddle. "That's a trick I'm going to teach my men. The newspapers don't lie about you, Mr. Fargo—you're trickier than a redheaded woman."

"No need to tack up bunting," Fargo warned him. "We've still got an all-night ride through unscouted country. Keep your wits about you, soldier blue. And you can start by reloading your weapons."

"Did I do all right, Mr. Fargo? That was my first skirmish."

Fargo was about to snap at the shavetail. Then he realized: A young man's first skirmish on the frontier *was* important.

"Lieutenant McKenna, you were some pumpkins, all right. You followed orders to the letter, stayed frosty under fire, and grouped your shots just right. Hell, I don't even believe you *went* to West Point."

Their mounts' bits were flecked with foam, so when Fargo deemed it safe both men swung down and walked the horses for twenty minutes to cool them out.

"You said this gent Corey Webster saved your life once," McKenna said as they led their mounts, "and paid a dear price for it. Was he scalped?"

"No Indians were in the mix. I was high in the Front Range of the Rockies—the Stony Mountains as Corey and other former mountain men still call them. I was still too green then to know how early the ice storms blew in from the north. One night the temperature fell so low and fast that I couldn't use my flint and steel to start a fire because my whole body was shaking too hard."

An owl hooted from somewhere close by and Fargo paused to make sure it was really an owl—Apaches used the owl hoot to signal.

"Anyhow," he resumed, "it commenced to snowing and it never stopped. I hobbled my horse inside a little declivity in the rocks and made myself a snow cave. After two days in that cold I was half out of my mind. I passed out somewhere along the third day. I came to inside a cabin in front of a roaring fire—just in time to see some tough old grizz amputating his own leg off just below the knee."

Wade McKenna's jaw slacked open in the moonlight. "Corey Webster?"

"His own self," Fargo affirmed. "Seems he was out on snowshoes looking for game and spotted my horse, half dead. He brought it back to the cabin but then started thinking he'd ought to look for its owner. It was still blue-ass cold, and by the time he found me he was frostbit himself. He figured me for gone beaver, but that didn't stop him from carrying me on his back for four miles to that cabin."

"Holy Toledo," McKenna said. "Four miles toting a big fellow like you?"

"I couldn't do it," Fargo said. "But somehow he did. But by the next morning his leg was turning black and he knew it was either the leg or his life. So that leather-tough son of a bitch drank a jug of potato whiskey, stuck a razor-sharp butcher knife into the fire, and hacked off his own pin."

A timber wolf howled mournfully, and the kid visibly shivered. "Damnation, Mr. Fargo! It's a wonder he didn't bleed to death."

"Oh, I helped with that much following his instructions. Used rope to tie a tourniquet above the knee while I packed flour around the wound to stem the flow. Then I bound it up good and stayed with him for a spell while he whittled his own peg. He used harness straps and buckles to attach it— still wears it today and gets around good. He's tougher than a two-bit steak."

"All that sacrifice for a stranger he found freezing in the snow," Wade marveled. "No wonder you admire him."

"Admire him? No, shavetail, a man *admires* a pretty girl. In my book, Corey Webster is ten inches taller than God."

"That hunch you mentioned earlier—you're afraid something has happened to him, aren't you?"

That was exactly what Fargo feared, but he had already said enough.

"Corey can take care of himself," Fargo said brusquely. "Now let's quit flapping our gums and use our eyes and ears. This ain't no Sunday stroll."

# 5

Throughout the rest of that long and arduous night the two riders followed the trail to Chimayo, climbing higher and higher into the Sangre de Cristo Range. They held their horses to a trot, a hard enough pace on an ascending ride. The air grew gradually thinner and colder until Fargo could see his and the Ovaro's breath forming white wraiths of steam. But man and beast welcomed the cold after the summer heat of the lower elevations.

At one point the trees cleared out and the two riders were surprised by a manada of wild horses breaking across the trail in front of them. They had to shorten their reins and pull back hard to keep their own mounts from joining them.

"Are they escaped horses?" Wade asked.

"Never been captives," Fargo replied. "They're descendants of the top-rate stock the Spanish explorers brought over. You'll find them all over New Mexico Territory and west Texas, especially around the Pecos River. If you can break one to leather, you'd have a horse that sells for five hundred dollars. But very few men can catch them."

Two hours before sunrise they encountered a choke point on the trail—boulders that had tumbled down from a steep slope on their left. With the slope on one side, and impenetrable tree cover on the other, Fargo cursed as he realized the only option. Both men rolled up their sleeves and wrestled each boulder aside until their horses could squeeze through.

"Now I see why the word 'travel' comes from 'travail,'" Wade punned as they hit leather.

Soon the trees thinned out and the trail leveled off as they reached the crown of the mountain. The new sun was a salmon-pink streak on the eastern horizon.

"Chimayo's about three miles ahead," Fargo said. "Corey's shack is another three miles outside the village. At least it's easy riding now."

The trail dipped and soon they entered a fertile valley surrounding a tight cluster of adobe buildings. Wild columbine colored the surrounding pastures and meadows with splashes of sky blue. Already the white-clad Pueblos were working the milpas, the communal fields. An old woman wrapped in a dark rebozo sat cross-legged in front of her hovel, crushing corn on a grinding stone.

"Peaceful-looking place," Wade remarked.

"Does your mother know you're out? This place is regularly sacked by Apaches, sometimes by Navajos and Comanches. Uncle Sam's blue-bloused soldiers are spread too thin to do much about it."

"They're supposed to," Wade insisted. "These people are wards of the New Mexico Territory."

"Fresh off ma's milk," Fargo said as he nudged the Ovaro up to a fast trot. "Your new commander in Santa Fe has a brother who manufactures weapons for the army. You think he wants peace and harmony out here?"

The few dwellings were of puddled adobe, the Indian style, with layers of grass-impregnated mud poured between forms. Even this poor excuse for a village had its solid adobe church with thick, buttressed walls. The only sound came from their echoing hoof clops and an old rotting windlass creaking like a rusty hinge in the breeze. The eerie noise goosebumped Fargo's forearms and reminded him of his "God fear" of last night.

Wade pointed toward a small pond beside the church. "Man alive, look at all those folks washing. They sure must like being clean. They're scrubbing themselves hard enough."

Fargo, eyes in shadow under his hat, followed the kid's finger. About two dozen Pueblos—men, women, and children—were scrubbing themselves with yucca root, creating a rich white lather. Seeing them, Fargo's lips formed a grim frown.

"They're not scrubbing off dirt," Fargo told the kid. "That's a religious ritual they mix in with their Christianity. There's been a murder and the entire village is now unclean."

"You don't think—"

31

"I don't think anything," Fargo cut him off. But his heels thumped the Ovaro up to a canter, then a lope.

Fewer than twenty minutes later they topped a long rise and spied a weather-beaten shack with a stovepipe chimney and a small pole corral out back.

"Only two scrubs in the corral," Fargo remarked tersely. "Corey usually has half a dozen or so. And there's fox furs drying on the racks outside—a man doesn't stretch furs until the heat of the day. Those were left out overnight."

"Hallo, the shack!" Fargo gave the hail as they rode in.

Even as Fargo swung down and tossed the reins forward, he reminded himself: Corey Webster was a tough old coot, all right, but he *was* old. Older than most men out west would ever get. If the legendary old mountain man had passed away of old age, it would sadden Fargo but it was also the natural cycle of life and death.

*They sure must like being clean. They're scrubbing themselves hard enough.*

*There's been a murder and the entire village is now unclean.*

Even before Fargo lifted the latchstring on the door he heard it: the high-pitched drone of flies, thousands of them in a feeding frenzy. He nudged the door open and felt his stomach bottom out at the sight. It was almost impossible to identify the corpse on the floor because of the shifting, writhing, blue-black blanket of flies covering it.

Face wrinkling at the stench, Fargo grabbed the horse blanket off the narrow cot and waved it through the flies, scattering many out the front door. Corey's head, part of his skull smashed in, emerged into view in the poor lighting. But it was the entrails, pulled from his body and stacked neatly on his chest, that shocked Fargo sick and silly.

His legs went rubbery. This was no longer a man—it was stew meat. Canister shot couldn't have butchered him worse.

Blood hammered in Fargo's temples, and he went numb from scalp to toes. In his mind's eye he saw himself waking up in another cabin and watching this brave man taking off his own leg—the hard price for saving Fargo's life. For a moment the shack went blurry, but he swiped at his eyes before tears could form. It wasn't the Trailsman's way to mourn with tears—his guns, his blade, his fists would balance the ledger.

"Mr. Fargo? Is everything all right?" McKenna called from outside.

Fargo swallowed hard to find his voice. His mouth felt dry and stuffed with cotton. "No, it ain't all right, kid. But come on in here. If you're going to be a soldier on the frontier, you'll need to get used to sights like this."

McKenna poked his head hesitantly around the door, one hand swiping away flies. When he saw the abomination on the floor, his face went moonstone white. "God-in-whirlwinds! Is that . . . ?"

"It was."

"But who did this?"

Fargo stepped outside to get away from the stench and the flies. "I'll tell you this much—a clan of crazy-drunk Comanches couldn't have butchered him worse."

That mess inside, Fargo told himself with numb frankness, had neither name nor soul. It was as if Satan himself had risen from hell to obliterate the old frontiersman.

"Your instincts were right, Wade," he admitted. "I should have followed your suggestion yesterday when we saw those four riders down in the valley. We *should* have challenged them because I think they did this. Just about the right number of scrubs are missing from the corral."

Fargo circled the shack slowly, reading sign in the sandy ground and in the trampled dirt of the corral. Several times he squatted and studied the ground intently for a long spell.

"Four men," he finally confirmed. "Two of them need boots bad judging from the cracks in the soles. One has hobnail boots in better condition, and he's a big, heavy man. See how his prints are deeper? None of these tracks is a day old yet."

"How can you tell that?" the young lieutenant asked.

"Take a close look at the edges of the prints. They're just starting to crumble."

Fargo stood up, his tanned face quietly dangerous. "It'll be turnabout soon enough for those four."

"You going to the authorities in Santa Fe?"

Fargo gave him a pitying look. "Do you really believe a

posse is going to ride all over Robin Hood's barn to catch the killers of a one-legged old man? They'll file a report and that'll be the end of it. It's up to me to square this."

The soldier's smooth-shaven face set itself in hard, determined lines. "And I'm going to side you."

"Like hob you will. Just like Corey I'm a one-man outfit, soldier blue. 'Sides, you got orders. You Bible-raised?"

McKenna nodded.

"Good. You can say a few words over him when we plant him. Corey told me once that he hated religion but loved the Lord."

Using Fargo's slicker, the two men brought Corey's body outside and buried it beside the shack. The officer solemnly recited the Lord's Prayer. Then Fargo covered the new grave with large rocks to keep off predators. By now both men, who had missed a night's sleep, were bone-weary.

"Their trail heads west. So we'll head that direction for a ways then make a cold camp and sleep for a few hours," Fargo decided. "Should be easy to cut sign on them. They might hightail it out of the territory altogether, but I doubt it. Most outlaws on the dodge around here head for Santa Fe. New faces aren't noticed there. Besides, I'm under orders to get you to your duty station."

"Soldiers are late all the time on the frontier," McKenna reminded him. "Besides, who's going to question the Trailsman? Let me side you, Mr. Fargo. I'm a good shot."

Fargo shook his head. "You're a damn good *young* man and I'd like to buy you a beer when you get older. Now quit pesticating and let's make tracks."

Fargo was right: The killers' trail was easy to follow. Although they avoided the main trail to Santa Fe, they took no pains to confuse any trackers. With about two hours of sunlight left, they reached a ranch house about twenty miles north of Santa Fe. Fargo saw four horses hobbled out front next to a buckboard.

"Let's check with these folks," he told McKenna. "You can see where the prints turn into that woods just past the fence. Matter fact," he added, knocking the riding thong off

his Colt, "maybe those four murdering bastards comman-
deered the house."

The two men hobbled their mounts in hawthorn bushes
beside the trail and drew their sidearms. They crept silently
up to the open front door of the house.

"Both of you Montoya boys admitted you was drunk as
the lords of creation," said a heavyset man with a craggy,
seamed face tanned nut brown. "I know how wild and crazy
that pulque can make a man. And everybody knows Judd
Sloan couldn't pay you much. Now fess up before I beat the
truth out of you yellow curs."

He was speaking to two young Mexican men who wore
the *chapajeros* of vaqueros. They were perched on sturdy
three-legged stools, heads slumped in dejection.

*"Vaya,* hombre, *es usted loco?"* demanded a breathtak-
ingly pretty Mexican woman standing beside the boys, her
dark eyes snapping sparks. "Sheriff Kinkaid, you must be
crazy to think Juan and Paco would kill the Sloans! Kill
women? And . . . and, *por Dios"*—she made the sign of the
cross—"butcher them?"

Still standing in the yard, guns leathered now, Fargo and
McKenna exchanged a startled glance.

Sheriff Hank Kinkaid, whom Fargo knew by reputation,
turned his attention to the woman. "Rosita, I ain't saying they
done it. Hell, Judd was found near a mile from here with a
bowie in his neck, and his womenfolk—well, Jesus, you seen
what was done to them. I got to dig into this. Tell me again
why you were here."

The pretty Mexican stamped her foot in frustration. She
wore a narrow-waisted gown and a lace mantilla. Fargo took in
the finely sculpted cheekbones, full, heart-shaped lips meant
for passionate kissing, and coffee brown, wing-shaped eyes.

"I have told it so many times you could set it to music! Juan
and Paco came into town yesterday for the fiesta. They became
so drunk they could not even sit their horses. I tied their mounts
to the back of Frank Tutt's buckboard and brought them back
here. It was late and I was very tired, so I pulled the buckboard
into the barn. I put some hay in the back of it and slept there.
*Es la verdad, lo juro.* I swear it is the truth."

"She's telling the truth, Sheriff Kinkaid," Fargo intervened, strolling into the house with Wade behind him. "Her brothers didn't do the killing."

Startled, Kinkaid filled his hand and pointed the Remington at Fargo. His Mexican deputy, who had been out of sight from the doorway, reluctantly drew and covered the soldier.

"Why? Did you?" Kinkaid demanded.

Fargo's lips twitched into a grin. "Hell, is my horse the next suspect?"

Kinkaid's deep-set, perceptive eyes bored into Fargo's. "Chuck the sass, buckskins. I wear the badge and I ask the questions. How do you know Juan and Paco are innocent?"

Fargo glanced left into the parlor. Blankets had been tossed over the victims. "Let me see the bodies and I'll tell you how."

"The hell you will. Ain't nobody gonna see them bodies, stranger. They was two fine women until yesterday. Now . . . well, I swear by all things holy, ain't *nobody* gonna see 'em."

"All right, just tell me this—were they butchered out? And when I say butchered, I mean by somebody who knows the trade."

The furrow between Kinkaid's silver eyebrows deepened in suspicion. "And just how would you know that? I see plenty of blood on the fringes of your buckskins."

"I know because they did the same to my friend Corey Webster near Chimayo. And the killers' trail leads here."

Kinkaid glanced at his deputy. "Corey Webster? Don't we know that name?"

The deputy, a neatly mustachioed man wearing a leather shako hat, nodded. "*Sí, Jefe.* He is the crusty old hombre who comes—came—to town to sell furs and horses each year. You arrested him one time for pissing in the street."

Kinkaid snorted. "Oh, yeah. The peg leg that told me to stick my"—he caught himself just in time, glancing toward Rosita—"my thingumajig in my ear and make a jug handle out of it."

"That would be Corey, all right," Fargo said, grinning fondly. He noticed that Rosita had been watching him since he stepped into the house, and Fargo liked the attention.

"I liked that tough old badger," Kinkaid told Fargo, "and

if you're telling the straight, I'm sorry your pard is dead. But—say, just who in the hell are you, anyway?"

Wade, who had stood silent all this time, now stepped formally forward, pulling his orders from his tunic.

"Sheriff, my name is Second Lieutenant Wade McKenna, newly attached to the Third Cavalry as assistant adjutant. This gentleman is Mr. Skye Fargo, currently under contract to the U.S. Army to lead a mapmaking expedition in the Department of New Mexico. He is also my official military escort and has been with me for the past ten days since we rode out from the Indian Territory. I can vouch for his actions during all that time."

The seams in Kinkaid's weathered face seemed to etch themselves deeper. "Vouch? Hell, boy, you're fresh out of three-corner britches."

"I'm a commissioned officer, sir, a commission signed by President Buchanan himself. If you are calling Mr. Fargo a murderer, then you're also calling me his accomplice. That is a libel, and by the articles of—"

"Put a stopper on your gob, tadpole, and put them damn papers away. I didn't accuse either one of you of a damn thing. If you—"

Kinkaid suddenly realized that his deputy, Rosita, and both of her brothers were staring at Fargo as if he were a talking dog.

"Skye Fargo, huh? Sure, the darling of the ink-slingers. The man who's always ducking the 'ultimate arrow,'" Kinkaid said sarcastically. "'A terrific sensation.'"

"Especially to the ladies," Rosita spoke up in a musical voice, sending Fargo a smoldering gaze he could feel in his hip pocket.

"Yeah, a whoremonger, too," Kinkaid barbed. "He don't look like so much to me, Pedro," he said to his deputy. "Matter fact, he's a mite whiffy. But even though he's a killer, I've never heard him called a murderer."

The sheriff and his deputy holstered their weapons. "Lissenup, Fargo. Like I said, I'm sorry about your old chum. I liked the old salt. But Chimayo comes under jurisdiction of the U.S. Marshal, and *this* crime is under my jurisdiction—especially since the killers will likely hole up in Santa Fe."

Fargo looked innocent as a newborn. "Of course. Did I ever gainsay that?"

"Not with your mouth, no. But I read about you in the crap sheets, and they all ballyhoo about how you come down like all wrath on anybody who harms your friends."

"Mr. Fargo has a very forgiving nature," Wade said from a deadpan.

"Ahuh. So do I. I forgive all my enemies—after I hang them."

Kinkaid took off his hat and mopped his brow with a sleeve. "Anyhow, *both* you jaspers best mark my words— interfering in an active case is a felony even in the territories. And you, soldier blue, could face a court-martial."

Fargo said, "Lieutenant McKenna reports for duty in Santa Fe immediately, sheriff. He won't be in your way."

"How 'bout you, Trailsman? What's your plan?"

"I'm s'posed to report to the army myself. There's a map-making expedition waiting on me."

"S'posed to?"

Fargo lifted one shoulder, his eyes meeting those smoldering dark gems of Rosita. He had seen that wordless invitation many times before: *Come thrill me, knave.*

"Haven't signed the contract yet," he finally replied.

"I strongly recommend that you do. I'm one stag you definitely don't want to clash with."

Fargo knew Kinkaid's reputation and wisely bit back his retort.

# 6

Kinkaid and his deputy moved into the lean-to bedroom at the back of the house.

"How 'bout you boys?" Fargo asked Juan and Paco. "Looks like you're out of a job now."

Juan, who appeared to be the oldest, nodded glumly. "We will stay for a time. Senor Sloan has a brother in—I cannot say this difficult name, but in a place in *Los Estados Unidos* that is very close to Canada. Now he is the *patrón* of this ranch. We will tend to the stock until his orders come."

Fargo shot a glance toward the back of the house. "You two found the women's bodies this morning, right?"

Both men nodded, faces grave.

"I have seen many hard things in Mexico." Juan said. "Things the Apaches did to my people, things the mind refuses to remember. But this thing with the senora and senorita—*ay, caramba!*"

"I saw them, too," Rosita chimed in. "I have little pity for *gringas*, but seeing them . . . Senor Fargo, I cannot call the killers animals for that would be an insult to animals."

"They were butchered, right?" Fargo pressed. "Their innards removed and stacked on their chests?"

*"Eso,"* Juan affirmed. "Exactly. But not *el patrón*. His horse dragged his body off."

"The men I'm looking for," Fargo said, "were riding Indian scrubs. Any sign of those?"

"We found four in the woods past the fence," Paco said. "All throat-slashed."

"So they must have stolen Sloan's horses. Do you know which ones are missing?"

"Two roans and two—*como se dice?*—coyote duns. Sometimes called lineback duns."

Fargo nodded before looking at Wade. "Coyote duns are favorite cow ponies with Mexican vaqueros. Good cutting horses and they're fast. And there must be a thousand roans in this area."

He turned to Juan again. "Did Mr. Sloan brand his horses?"

"His riding horses, *sí*. But not his work stock. Even his cattle are not branded because they are not free-range. He meant to do so when the herd increased."

"What's with all the damn questions, Fargo?" Kinkaid's gravelly voice demanded. He had sneaked back into the room. "You toting a badge now?"

"Just curious, Sheriff."

"Ahuh." Those perceptive, penetrating eyes skewered Fargo. "Curious is just the word. And you know what it done to the cat."

Kinkaid tilted his head toward the open door. "Light a shuck out of here, both of you. And keep your damn noses out of the pie. We got two newspapers in town, Fargo. Why'n't you go primp for them—after you take a goddamn bath. Both you two smell like a whorehouse at low tide."

McKenna bristled at this. "Look, Sheriff, we've been in the saddle since—"

Fargo touched his shoulder. "Never mind, Lieutenant. The sheriff is right. The stench coming off us could raise blood blisters on new leather."

Out in the yard, Fargo scowled at the kid. "Get off your high horse, junior. You ain't back in the Land of Steady Habits now. Out west, a man has to pick his battles carefully. If you try to fight over every trifling insult, you'll end up having your mail delivered by moles. Those gold bars of yours cut no ice with him."

"A good point, Mr. Fargo, and I'm caught upon it."

"That's not all. I'm going to be locking horns with Kinkaid before this Corey deal is over. I hear brains ain't his strong suit, but he's got enough guts to fill a smokehouse. And he's mule-stubborn. No point in getting him on the peck before I have to."

Fargo and McKenna hadn't quite reached the road before a feminine voice pulled them up short.

"Senor Fargo! *Un momento, por favor.*"

Rosita hurried out of the house to join them. "May I speak with you . . . privately?" she added, glancing at Wade.

"Uhh . . . I'll knock the hobbles off the horses," he muttered, scurrying off.

"Please forgive my boldness," she told Fargo, her wing-shaped eyes meeting his frankly. "You see, I can read the *Norteamericano* newspapers, and often they write of you. And then, when you came into the house just now . . . well, *I* think you smell good, like a man who *lives* like a man. And you are so—how does one say?—so *guapo.*"

"Handsome," Fargo supplied the English word, swallowing the flattery effortlessly.

"This, yes. I know I am shameless, but a woman in my position cannot afford to be modest. Do you find me desirable enough to come . . . visit me?"

Fargo's intense eyes swept her body from the masses of jet-black hair to the perfectly turned ankles, especially noticing the ample bosom so characteristic of Mexican women. They returned to those ripe-berry lips and their promise of juicy kisses.

"You're pretty as four aces," he told her, "with a wild card left over. I think a . . . visit might be good for both of us."

"Oh, I promise it will," she told him, her voice going husky. "But I must tell you the truth. I am not married, but I am the woman—*one* of the women—of Frank Tutt."

"I've heard of him. He owns the Gilded Cage, the most popular gambling house in Santa Fe."

She nodded. "Perhaps you have not heard that he is a mean man—and a jealous one. He takes any woman who—how do you say?—captures his sight."

"Catches his eye?"

"*Preciso.* But all of his women must be faithful or . . . or he makes them very sorry."

"Look," Fargo said regretfully, "we could make some beautiful music together, but if it's going to cause you—"

"He can go to hell! I have tricked him before, and it is easy. He sleeps each day until sunset, then begins to gamble downstairs with his, how you say, crooked friends. They gamble until dawn. You must only ride through the alley behind the Gilded Cage and look for a lamp I will set on my window ledge. There are stairs in the back. I will unlock the door at the top of the stairs."

"It's always the lady's choice," Fargo surrendered without much of a struggle. "When?"

"Not tonight. I did not return last night, and Tutt will be angry. The sheriff is going to tell him what happened, but still I must be careful this night. But tomorrow night ride through the alley and watch for the light. If you think I am shameless now, wait until then."

By now McKenna had led both horses onto the trail and held them by the bridle reins.

"What did she want?" he asked curiously as Fargo stepped up into leather.

He gave the kid a long look, shaking his head. "She gave me her recipe for corn tortillas."

"Hunh. Funny thing to give a man. Nice of her though."

"She's generous to a fault," Fargo agreed. "Look, Wade, just keep riding until we're out of sight behind the woods. I want to verify something without that damn Kinkaid seeing me."

When they were safely out of sight, Fargo swung down and threw his reins forward. Wade joined him.

For a long time Fargo squatted on his heels to study the trail, first studying the dirt closely and then shifting to a new spot.

"They headed to Santa Fe, all right," he verified. "They mean to hole up there."

Wade shook his head in confusion. "I don't get it. This trail is covered with horseshoe prints and wagon ruts. How can you tell the right ones?"

"It's easy if you're patient. We know about when they left Chimayo, and we know how long it takes to get here. That means the prints should be about a day old by now. Day-old prints have usually started to crumble but they're still visible. So I ignore the fresh prints and the ones clearly older than a day."

Fargo pointed to a line of prints. "The trail is wide here and they left four abreast. After what these buzzards did to the Sloan family, you'd expect them to be in a puffin' hurry, and they were. These four sets of prints are about three-and-a-half feet apart—that's a gallop. Most of these other prints overlap—that's a walk or a trot, the usual pace on a trail like this."

"Holy Jehoshaphat! I got none of that at West Point."

Fargo stood up. "I got it from Corey Webster. Among other things that have saved my bacon over the years. Well, listen—the horses are tired and so are we. It's still twenty miles into Santa Fe, and it's too late for you to report to the military liaison office anyway. Let's pitch a camp up ahead and ride in come morning."

The two men found a sheltered copse about two miles farther on. There was no water, but the bladder bag tied to Fargo's saddle horn was full. They shared beef jerky and a can of peaches.

"You ever heard of anything like this?" Wade asked. "I mean, butchering people like they were cattle and piling up the guts in a neat package?"

"Nothing quite like this," Fargo admitted. "Certain tribes will mutilate their victims although most learned it from the Spanish. I've seen dead soldiers with their pizzles cut off and stuffed in their mouths, eyes cut out and placed on nearby rocks, that type of deal. But nothing like this bunch."

Suddenly, in Fargo's mind, the steady drone of insects transformed itself into the obscene feeding frenzy of flies inside Corey's shack. For the space of a few heartbeats rage boiled up inside him like a tight bubble escaping, and it felt like a hot knife was twisting deep in his guts.

Mercifully, the kid said something.

"What's that?" Fargo said.

"I sure wish you'd let me side you. I know Mr. Webster was your friend, not mine, but I feel like I know him. And then look at that poor family—I feel like I'm part of this thing."

"I know how you feel, Wade, and I don't blame you. You're a decent man and you want to see justice done. But on a deal like this I work best alone. Besides, if you think Major

Bruce Harding would ever give you permission to mix into a civilian crime like this—well, wait until you meet him."

"I guess you're right," McKenna said, a disappointed edge to his voice. "Anyhow, what is Santa Fe like? Will these killers be easy to spot there?"

Fargo mulled that one. Santa Fe was home to fabulous wealth but also plenty of mean, dirty, lazy men who looked out at the world from lidded eyes and surly faces. It was overflowing with criminals on the dodge, and trying to guess which ones murdered Corey and the Sloans would be like trying to find a sliver in an elephant's ass.

"Nothing's easy in Santa Fe," he finally replied, "except getting bucked out in smoke."

# 7

Much of the nation had been left destitute and cash-starved by the Depression of '59. But Santa Fe remained a frontier oasis and boomtown, prosperous as a pretty whore at the end of the trail. Signs all over the city advertised HELP WANTED, although some added in parentheses ORPHANS PREFERRED.

"The place sure is busy," Wade remarked as he and Fargo trotted down the wide central street.

"Always is," Fargo assured him. "This is the northern terminal for The King's Highway, El Camino Real. That's a trade route that stretches way the hell down into the Internal Provinces of Mexico, places like Aguascalientes and Guadalajara. New merchant caravans leave every week or so. There's jaspers in this town who got money to toss at the birds."

Despite Fargo's cheery tone, his wary, shaded eyes stayed in constant motion. He watched doorways, alley entrances. The mostly adobe buildings were plastered white and topped by red tile roofs. Wade seemed fascinated as he watched Indian women making the tiles, forming them on their thighs to ensure uniformity.

"That low, long building on the right," Fargo said, "is El Palacio. Most locals call it the Mud Palace. It's the oldest government house on American soil."

"Hell, I thought it was a stable. Is everything in this city made of mud?"

"Everything except some newer hotels and the mansions on College Street. But don't high-hat the architecture, kid. This place will never burn to the ground like cities back in the States. Well, here we are—the Department of New

45

Mexico Military Liaison Office. Better brush the grass off your blouse. This Major Harding is a rule book commando."

They reined in at a modest-looking building with the crossed sabers of the Third Cavalry Regiment painted on the plank door. Both men swung down and wrapped their reins around the tie rail.

"So this is where I'll be posted instead of in the field," the kid said glumly. "It's a brevet or a coffin for most cavalrymen— me, I get a damn quill and a pot of ink. Assistant to the adjutant, my sweet aunt!"

Fargo sympathized with the young officer. Camp Rio Grande, twenty miles south of Santa Fe near the village of Madrid, was home to the Third Regiment. But it was a rustic outpost and all administrative duties were performed here in the territorial capital.

"Buck up, shavetail," he said as they headed for the door. "In six months you can put in for a transfer. Meantime, this city is ripe with beautiful women of every race. You just might get to like it."

"Fargo, timely met," called out an officer sitting at a desk covered with maps. "I've got a six-man team all provisioned and champing at the bit to get up into those mountains."

Wade, well-schooled in the military protocols, came sharply to attention in front of his superior's desk. "Sir! Second Lieutenant Wade McKenna reporting for duty!"

Major Bruce Harding was a small, neat, worried-looking man who constantly rubbed one knuckle across his mustache, smoothing it. He did so now as he cast a skeptical eye over his new assistant.

"I know you've been in transit, mister," he said in a harsh tone. "But isn't a sadiron part of your military issue?"

"Yessir, but—"

"Keep your 'butts' in your pocket, mister! That sadiron can be heated over a campfire and used to press your uniform. And, Christ Jesus, you smell like a manure pile."

Fargo grinned as he plopped down onto a ladder-back chair, marveling at the petty nature of military life and glad he'd never taken the oath. Harding left Wade at attention as he turned to Fargo.

"Can you leave today?" he demanded. "The War Department is eager to get at that band of Jicarilla Apaches who have holed up in the Sangre de Cristos. But we can't put troops in those mountains without maps."

Fargo shook his head. "Sorry, Major. You'll either have to hire a new scout or hold the expedition for a while."

"Surely, man, you can't be serious?" Harding's knuckle fairly flew over his mustache now. "Wait. I know your reputation. Is it a woman?"

"Nothing so pleasant. In case you don't know, there's a gang of four killers roaming this area. Not just killers—at least one of them is butchering out their victims. Leaving their guts piled on top of them."

Harding waved this aside as if he were shooing a fly. "You're behind times, Fargo. The army has known about this bunch for days. In fact, we had them in custody briefly."

Fargo leaned forward in his chair. "Had them in custody?"

"Yes. By sheer chance, one of our mountain patrols caught them red-handed murdering two prospectors in the Manzano Mountains down south near Bosque Farms. The patrol left them behind under a military guard, just two sentries. Somehow they overpowered the guards and escaped—but not before killing and butchering the soldiers. We found two carbines washed ashore at Crying Woman Creek. It's more like a deep, fast river this season, and they must have lost them while fording."

"Are there any living soldiers who can describe these men?" Fargo asked.

"If there are, they can't be summoned. That mountain patrol is dogging Apaches, and by now they're likely way the hell down in the Dragoon Mountains."

Harding said all this impatiently as if something more near and dear to his heart was on his mind. His next remark confirmed this.

"Fargo, these killers are not your responsibility. Sheriff Kinkaid and the U.S. marshal will handle this. Your obligation is to the American citizens—these Apaches are vicious cutthroats who must be exterminated."

"Apaches are no boys to fool with," Fargo agreed. "But I doubt there's any holing up in the Sangre de Cristo Range.

They raid into these parts, but they left these ranges long ago for the mountains in southern Arizona or Mexico."

Harding's face seemed suddenly etched in granite. "Multiple reports say you're wrong."

Fargo despised this martinet and his phony reports. False reports about "Indian scares" were common because they stirred up settlers. Stirred-up settlers meant more soldiers, and thus, more lucrative contracts to opportunists like Harding's brother back in the settlements. Jeremy Harding was a master gunsmith with his own factory and he was making a small fortune by arming the spirit of westward expansion.

But Fargo let all that go. Right now he didn't give a frog's fat ass about the politics of profiteering.

"All right, Major, so I'm wrong. It doesn't matter. I sign no contracts until I hunt these skunk-bit coyotes down and kill them."

"Since when did you become a vigilante?"

"Since they killed and butchered a friend of mine near Chimayo."

Harding's lips twitched with the effort to keep the scorn off them. "I didn't realize you were such a sentimentalist. Surely you've lost plenty of friends over the years?"

"Not like this one."

Harding heaved a sigh of surrender. He had learned long ago that trying to change Skye Fargo's mind was like trying to change the weather.

"All right," he said. "I'll try to hold command off as long as possible. They insist on having you along."

"Sir?" Wade McKenna piped up. "Permission to speak?"

"What?"

"Permission to be assigned to temporary additional duty so I can accompany Mr. Fargo."

"Lieutenant, are you a bigger fool than God made you? I can't stop Fargo from bucking the law, he's a civilian. But the army has no authority in this matter. We are restrained by law from getting involved in civilian law enforcement."

"Yessir, but I would just be an assistant. And with help, Mr. Fargo can get his job done quicker and turn to the map-making expedition."

Harding gave the upstart a quelling stare. "Clean your

ears or cut your hair, you soft-brained fool. You are a staff officer, not a scout or prison chaser. Besides, Fargo doesn't carry sugar tits for infants."

Fargo wanted no help for this hunt. But he despised an officer who abused his men as Harding did and he couldn't resist this chance to thwart him.

"Actually, Major," he spoke up, "Lieutenant McKenna may have neglected to press his blouse, but he has more starch in his collar than you credit him with. I could use his help. Think of it as field training for the lad."

Harding looked like he was trying to swallow a nail sideways. "Jesus, Fargo, you know the realities of frontier soldiering. This is summer—a third of our enlisted men have taken French leave."

Fargo nodded. French leave was a euphemism for deserting. Every winter men enlisted for food and shelter and then many deserted with spring thaw.

"The snowbirds fly every summer," Fargo conceded. "Not too many men want to put their bacon in the fire for three hots and a cot. Especially in Apache country. But Lieutenant McKenna won't be deserting. Besides, you can spare a quill merchant for a spell."

Harding shook his head. "Out of the question."

Fargo played his hole card. "Is Colonel Peatross around? I haven't chewed the fat with him lately."

A sea change came over Harding's stubborn face. It was widely known that Fargo's clever diversion of a Sioux war party, back in the Black Hills, had saved Andrew Peatross and his regiment from certain slaughter. Since then, anything Fargo wanted he got.

"McKenna, your orders will be cut immediately," Harding gave in. "But you are to engage in no activities contraindicated by official army regulations. Is that clear?"

"Absolutely, sir."

"You will wear your uniform at all times—is that also clear?"

"Perfectly, sir."

Fargo suppressed a sly grin. "As I understand it, Major, a man on temporary additional duty is entitled to per diem pay."

"Fargo, this is outright blackmail!"

"That's an ugly word, sir. I call it going by the book."

Harding spread both arms in a gesture of surrender. "You'll be authorized five dollars a day, Lieutenant. The disburser in the rear of the building will give you a government chit. By law it must be honored by all legal merchants. But try to stay under your spending limit."

"That's the patriotic thing to do," Fargo said solemnly as he stood up. "I'll keep a close eye on him, Major."

"I know you will," the officer replied in a deadpan voice. "That's what I'm worried about."

Santa Fe was crawling with livery stables, but Fargo had learned from woeful experience that many charged for oats and then fed the horses hay. The one he preferred was just past the southern outskirts of the city, owned by an honest old Mexican named Manuel.

"A rubdown and a currycomb for both horses," Fargo instructed the old man as he and Wade stripped the leather from their mounts. "They've made a long ride and they'll need extra grain for a couple days. The sorrel is used to being stalled nights but—"

"Turn the fine Ovaro out into the paddock," Manuel recited from memory. "No stallion is content in a stall all night. Too much wild in them."

Fargo grinned. The years had seamed the old man's face but not his memory. Fargo and Wade carried the saddles and bridles into the tack room, tossing the saddles onto wooden racks and hanging the bridles on coffee cans nailed to the wall.

Manuel spoke in Spanish to the *mozo*, an *indio* lad of about twelve years named Benito. The boy gladly tossed aside the harness he was mending and began rubbing down the Ovaro.

"Manuel," Fargo said, "do you mind if I look at the rest of the horses?"

"*Por que no?* Why not? The eyes can do no harm, I think maybe."

There were six horses shaking out the kinks in the paddock, a dozen more in the stalls. Fargo spent a minute studying those in the paddock, then walked up and down the livery looking at the rest.

"Just like I feared," he told Wade. "Out of eighteen horses, seven are linebacks and four are roans. We're just pissing into the wind."

Manuel was in the tack room pounding caulks into horseshoes. Fargo joined him.

"*Viejo*, have you had four men drop their horses off here lately? Rough customers on linebacks and roans?"

The old man shook his head. "But there are eleven livery stables in town."

"I know, and the criminals know which ones to use, right?"

"*Como no*, of course. Many are owned by criminals themselves. If a horse has been stolen, they will provide false—how you say?—Williams of sale."

Fargo chuckled. "Bills of sale."

"This, yes. Often they trade a horse for the stolen one and quickly move them down to Albuquerque or Madrid. I fear you will have little luck trying to find stolen horses in the City of Holy Faith. This is a criminal's paradise, I think maybe."

"Well," Fargo told his young companion, "both of us could use a bath and a hot meal. I drew a month's pay when we left Medicine Creek, and that per diem of yours is burning a hole in my pocket. Let's go get a room."

"Yeah, then I can finally get this uniform cleaned and pressed."

"Sure, but then just hang it up. You'll be in mufti for this job."

"Mufti? But you heard Harding—I mean, Major Harding. He gave me a direct order to stay in uniform."

"Harding doesn't know shit from apple butter. Anyway, a field commander can override a superior's order if the situation deems it. And right now I'm your field commander, eh? That uniform of yours is pretty, all right, but it's an easy target for dry gulchers."

Boot heels drumming along the boardwalk, saddlebags hanging from their shoulders, both men kept their eyes in motion as they headed toward the Dorsey House in the middle of town.

"You know," Wade said, "unless those four scum buckets read that letter you sent to Corey, they shouldn't know you're in town. Even if they read it, they can't know when you're arriving."

"Good point," Fargo said, brightening a bit. "It's always good to have the element of surprise on your side."

Up ahead, a printer's devil was pasting the latest broadsheets from the *Santa Fe New Mexican* to a wall. Fargo glanced at it in passing, then froze in place gaping at the screaming headline:

SKYE FARGO, FAMOUS TRAILSMAN, VISITS
SANTA FE ON BLOODY VENGEANCE QUEST!!!

"I can always count on the ink slingers to cut me off at the knees," Fargo carped, not even bothering to read the story. "Sheriff Kinkaid did that on purpose to gum up the works. So much for the element of surprise."

Fargo noticed a rough frontier type weaving in their direction, obviously carrying a brick in his hat. Either by accident or intention, he jostled Wade hard in passing.

"Hey, mister!" Wade shouted after him. "You need to learn some damn manners!"

The drunk stopped and did an unsteady about-face. "Zat so, you little pin dick toy soldier? Mebbe you're just the boy to learn me some, uh?"

"Let it go, kid," Fargo advised. "That hombre looks double rough."

But Wade, full of the dignity of a new officer, had blood in his eyes. The man walked back and squared off in front of the soldier. Fargo watched Wade's eyes go steely with purpose and winced, knowing what was coming. Without warning, the drunk connected with a haymaker that knocked Wade to the ground.

Fargo had deliberately stayed out of it, letting the kid learn at the school of hard knocks. But when the man pulled a bowie with a twelve-inch blade from his waistband, Fargo moved like a coiled spring, pulling the intimidating Arkansas toothpick from its boot sheath.

"Do it, friend, and you'll be shoveling coal in hell," Fargo warned him. "You made your point, now give over."

The man appraised Fargo's weather-seasoned face, bloody

buckskins, and no-nonsense knife. He put his knife away. "I didn't plan to kill the little titty baby, mister. Just leave a little scar on his pretty face to remind him he ain't living in no storybook."

Fargo grinned. "I believe you. But that haymaker you gave him has sent this lad to school, and I'd wager he'll learn his lessons."

Wade groaned and sat up, looking for the stagecoach that ran over him.

The man nodded. "Hell, I was young wunst, too, and done stupid shit like that. 'Sides, you look like a good man to leave alone," he said to Fargo before walking away.

"Did I get any licks in?" Wade asked as Fargo helped him to his feet.

"He popped you over like a ninepin," Fargo scoffed. "Listen, you better write this on your pillowcase: You've got to stop signaling your intention in your eyes. Don't mirror a damn thing. Strike like a rattlesnake, just like he did. Better yet, what did I just tell you at the Sloan place? Don't get on the peck just because a drunk jostles you."

"What if it had been you he ran into?"

"It's happened plenty. If a man's drunk, and a jostle is as far as it goes, I just overlook it. On the frontier you don't run into trifling danger. You have to pick your fights carefully or you won't make it to thirty."

Still rubbing his jaw, Wade nodded. "I take your point. Like the fight we're in now."

Suddenly Fargo heard it again: the obscene buzzing of flies in Corey's shack. His jaw set itself hard. "Yeah. Just like the fight we're in now."

# 8

It was Fargo's usual custom, on the rare occasions when he didn't sleep under the stars, to stay in cheap boardinghouses and roach-pit hotels. But he had heard about the legendary Dorsey House, located on Santa Fe's Calle Linda, in every corner of the West.

"You know, Wade," he said as they strolled the boardwalk, "I'm flush right now and you got Uncle Sugar's chit that no business can refuse by law. Besides, we got four killers that know we're in town, and it's not likely they'll be looking for us in the lap of luxury. Let's go snooks on a room at the Dorsey."

"I never heard of the place but that's jake by me, Mr. Fargo. But, you know, we don't know these killers from any of the other riffraff in town. They know us from your buckskins and my uniform. They could have a spy on us right now."

"Reg'lar sunshine peddler, ain't you?" Fargo groused, but once again the kid was right.

Five minutes later Wade stood gawking like a rube at the Dorsey's elegant lobby. The hand-hewn hemlock beams had been transported cross-country from Pennsylvania. A magnificent carved cherrywood staircase rose in a dizzying spiral toward a walnut cathedral ceiling aglitter with crystal chandeliers. Canaries in gilt cages sent up a melodious chorus.

"Man alive!" Wade marveled, his eyes wide to take all of it in. "This is the frontier? It looks like Napoleon's palace."

"If old fuss-and-feathers Harding could see you now," Fargo said, "he'd have a conniption."

Wade looked innocent. "You're my field commander, sir. Do you order me to stay here?"

"Strict orders," Fargo assured him although his attention had just been diverted to the center of the lobby. A group of elegantly dressed young ladies shared a huge circular sofa with a central headrest. They had obviously just arrived by stagecoach—one of them was complaining bitterly about the trail dust coating her new silk taffeta gown. A couple of them cast curious eyes toward the rugged man in buckskins and his soldier companion. One copper-haired coquette sent Fargo a bold come-hither look from behind a sequined fan.

Fargo was cautious here, for at nearby reading tables with green-shaded gas lamps their fashionably dressed husbands and fathers smoked cigars and commented on stories in the country's major newspapers. Few of them deigned to notice the dusty new arrivals—as did the hotel's gaudily uniformed staff.

Fargo spotted one lass watching him when she thought he wasn't looking—a remarkable beauty who rated aces high even in Fargo's vast samples. She was simply dressed in a dark calico skirt and white shirtwaist; this only emphasized even more her China blue eyes offset by a golden waterfall of hair tumbling down over her shoulders in a lush confusion.

"Is she a goddess?" Wade wondered aloud.

"Nope, just one fine specimen of woman flesh," Fargo replied. "And once I smell a little better, I aim to make her acquaintance."

"When that hot little firecracker Rosita gets done with you," Wade teased, "you may not be walking for a while."

"Son, you *are* a quick study. Well, let's go dicker with that desk clerk smirking at us."

They crossed to a marble counter and flopped their saddlebags onto it. This earned a disdainful frown from a slope-shouldered man even taller than Fargo but string-bean skinny.

"Our bathhouse out back is open to the public," he hinted pointedly. "You men will find more affordable quarters in the north section of town."

"Oh, we'd like to stay here," Fargo said amiably.

"I'm afraid that's out of the question. Only the finer elements of society are allowed at the Dorsey."

Fargo could sense the hotheaded Wade starting to bristle

and gave him a poke with his elbow. The kid remembered his lesson and calmed down.

"We're on official military business," Wade lied, pulling out his per diem chit. "As you know, this document must be accepted by law."

The clerk glommed it and heaved a disconsolate sigh. "I have to accept you by law, Lieutenant, but not your friend here."

"Mr. Fargo and I are on a joint mission."

Hearing the name, the clerk reacted as if he'd been scalded. Fargo could have shot Wade for mentioning his name.

"Fargo? Well, yes, just today I read . . . that's a different matter, gentlemen. Would you like adjoining rooms? They're eight dollars each a night, breakfast included."

Wade almost choked. Clean hotel rooms could be had all over the West for two dollars.

"We'd like to go easy on the government," Fargo interceded. "How about one room with two beds?"

"Certainly. Please sign the register."

Fargo pulled a gold dollar from his pocket and planked it on the counter. "That gorgeous blonde sitting on the sofa—happen to know her name?"

The clerk hesitated but the dollar held his eyes. "Leora Padgett. She just checked in with her father, Henry. He's a merchant from Albany, New York."

Fargo planked another dollar. "Does she have a husband or a beau?"

"No husband. She signed her name as 'Miss Padgett.' But I hardly think . . . I mean, she seems a very proper young lady."

"Reg'lar goddess," Fargo agreed, grinning at Wade before heading back toward the bathhouse.

"Your friend is wasting his time," the clerk told Wade. "She's not only beautiful. She's very refined and from a wealthy family. I hardly think an uncouth ruffian in buckskins would interest her."

Wade picked up the key. "Think so? Fargo will get her naked. He's the Trailsman."

A Chinese kid, wearing a floppy blue blouse and his hair in long pigtails, poured another bucket of hot water into Fargo's tub. The Trailsman luxuriated in the soapy water perfumed with rose petals, feeling his trail-weary muscles relaxing. But he had his back to a wall and his eyes constantly on the door, and his Colt lay within easy reach.

"Listen," he told Wade, who occupied the next tub, "a hotel desk clerk can be your best friend or your worst enemy. I don't trust this one, so let's not poke fire with a sword."

"Yeah, I realized that just in time. He knows right where we are. I wonder if those four killers do."

"They're a greasy-sack outfit but that kind can be dangerous. Thanks to Kinkaid shooting off his mouth to the newspaper, our location won't be a secret for very long."

Fargo dried himself and changed into his spare buckskins. By now the Chinese kid had cleaned and polished his boots and brushed off his hat. Fargo slipped him four bits in silver. When he turned and spotted Wade his lips twitched into a grin. The kid wore a rust-colored sack suit and a stiff felt derby.

"Let me guess: You were a drummer of ladies' notions before you joined the army."

"I'm not a Western man, Mr. Fargo. This is how we dress back in Cleveland."

"You look fine, sprout. I'm just roweling you. That conk cover won't do on the frontier, though. Brim's too narrow."

They had to cross the lobby to reach the stairs. Most of the men had retired to the hotel bar, but the women had remained. Fargo saw Leora Padgett and the copper-haired coquette seated at the writing desks composing letters.

"I'll be up in a minute," Fargo told his companion, combing his wet hair with his fingers. He felt the tall, skinny clerk's eyes on him as he crossed to the desk beside Leora's and took a seat, picking up a copy of *Leslie's Illustrated Weekly* and beginning to leaf through it.

Her hyacinth perfume wafted to his nostrils.

"Miss," he said out of the blue, "I wish I was a painter."

She hung fire for a moment, for proper ladies did not speak

with men to whom they hadn't been introduced. But curiosity got the better of her.

"I beg your pardon."

"Well, if I was an artist I would paint your portrait. Then, anytime I wanted a reminder of what beauty is, I'd study it."

She blushed deep to the roots of her golden hair. "Sir, you're being forward."

"I am," Fargo agreed. "But that's better than being backward."

In spite of herself, Leora smiled at his pun.

Copper hair said, "Don't let her fool you. She noticed you the moment you walked into the hotel. Her name is Leora. And you must be Skye Fargo—the beard, the eyes, the bullet holes in your hat."

"Constance," Leora objected, "Mr. Fargo knows who he is."

Fargo opened his mouth to speak but an irritated male voice beat him to it.

"Leora, come along to dinner," said a stout, muttonchopped man in his early forties. He aimed a disapproving glance at Fargo. "Sir, I intend no offense, but I'd appreciate it if you stay away from my daughter."

"I take no offense," Fargo assured him. "And if Leora is under twenty-one, I'll honor your request."

"She's twenty-three," Constance piped up.

Fargo stood up. "In that case," he said politely to her father, "it's up to your daughter."

"That remains to be seen," Padgett huffed as Fargo walked off.

Up in the room he found Wade gawping at the splendor of their quarters. "Man alive! You couldn't find finer digs than this in Manhattan!"

Fargo took in the gold-gilt mirrors, fireplaces mantled and faced with blood onyx, marble, and slate. Between the two beds with ruffled coverings was a fancy velvet pull-rope for summoning a bellboy.

"Maybe later I'll order up a bottle of who-shot-john," Fargo said, slinging his saddlebag into a corner. "I wish now we hadn't locked up our rifles at the livery."

"I think we're safe in this hotel," Wade said.

"Sure, and did you ever see an oyster walk upstairs? Listen, hayseed, don't let all this civilized luxury fool you. There's four killers out there most likely planning to get in the first lick."

Fargo decided to stretch out for a little nap before venturing out later to see if the pretty Rosita had placed a lantern in her window. As he unbuckled his shell belt, Wade went to the window.

"Mite stuffy in here," the kid said.

"Stand to one side of that window, boy," Fargo snapped. "Do you even know gee from haw?"

The last word was still on Fargo's lips when shards of glass rocketed inward and a shot rang out below. Wade's stiff derby flew off his head and he dove for the floor even as a geyser of plaster dust erupted from the wall behind Fargo.

Fargo, with the reflexes of a cat, was covered down before the hat hit the floor. "You hit?" he called out.

"No, but great day in the morning! I think I have a new part in my hair."

Fargo filled his hand with blue steel and edged up to one side of the window, peering out. In the late-afternoon sun he saw nothing but a service alley and a grassy lot beyond it.

"The shooter decided to rabbit," he said. "Jesus, kid, do I have to powder your butt and tuck you in? Didn't they teach you anything about cover and concealment at West Point?"

"Sure, but not in hotel rooms."

"Harken and heed—you and me are targets now until we toss the net around these plug-uglies. You shoulda taken that desk job today. You were one inch away just now from getting knocked out from under your hat by a bullet."

"Yeah, a brand-new hat with a bullet hole in it." Wade climbed to his feet.

"I sniff a rat here," Fargo said. "A tall beanpole of a rat. Those killers sure as shit got our room location in a hurry."

"The clerk?"

"It sure's hell wasn't a little bird that told them. I knew that damn clerk was bent. C'mon, we're gonna straighten him out."

The lobby was nearly deserted when they reached it.

"Stand to my right," Fargo told Wade. "Block the view."

Fargo plastered a smile on his face as he approached the

**59**

desk. The clerk watched him uncertainly. In an eyeblink Fargo had reached across the marble counter, grabbed the man's shirt front, and hauled him halfway over the counter. Quicker than thought Fargo produced his Arkansas toothpick and pressed the lethal point into the clerk's jugular vein.

"Lissenup, you little perfumed barber's clerk, and lissenup good. You're going to assign us a new room, savvy that? And if you tell one swinging dick where we are, I'm going to open you up from neck to nuts. This ain't chin music—it's a pure-dee promise. Have we got an understanding?"

The clerk's voice sounded like a sucking drain. "But, sir, I didn't—"

"In a pig's ass!"

Fargo's powerful arms pulled the clerk up farther. He moved the point of the knife down to his crotch. "You may think you're a rooster now, but one slice from this toothpick and you're a capon—*comprende?*"

"Cuh-cuh-*comprendo.*"

"Jesus," Wade hissed, "he's pissed himself!"

Fargo flung the clerk back behind the counter. "Now tell me—the hombre who paid you for our room number. What did he look like?"

"A—a little fellow with shifty eyes. Pockmarked face. Wore range clothes too big for him."

Fargo flashed the knife again. "Now you give us a new room. And remember this—I ain't one to chew my cabbage twice. Any more trouble from you, I'll gut you like a fish."

Later, in their new room on a different floor, Fargo met McKenna's eyes. "Don't be fooled by how easy I handled that clerk. From here on out cover your ampersand—we're in for six sorts of hell."

# 9

Three·miles southwest of Santa Fe, on the old federal freight road to Rio Ranchos, a nearly invisible trail led off the road and through a series of rocky gullies to the long-deserted ruins known as Los Hornos or The Ovens. At one time a Pueblo Indian village, the residents had been slain or driven off by Cortez and his conquistadors. Most of the dwellings had crumbled with time, leaving only the sturdy outdoor ovens.

Since the Mexican War, however, it had become an occasional outlaw haven, and a flimsy shack had been built from wagon wood and canvas. Ray Nearhood, who hailed from New Mexico Territory and once rode with a gang known as the Young Turks, knew of the place and led Ulrick and the rest to it.

"Jed, you stupid shit," Baylis Ulrick fumed in the dying light outside the shack, "why in Sam Hill did you shoot from that distance with a mother-lovin' handgun? They was four stories up! I told you to take the Volcanic with you."

Longstreet had just returned from his botched mission. "Hell, boss, I'm a poor hand with a long gun. 'Sides, that's a busy part of town. Aiming a rifle draws more attention than just snapping a bead with a short iron."

Baylis mulled that for a minute and nodded. "That shines. And you done a damn good job of switching out them stolen horses. Won't nobody be looking for these mounts we got now."

All four men were in a holiday mood. Their sacking of the Sloan ranch house had turned up three hundred dollars in gold and silver, two Colt Navy handguns, and a Greener 12-gauge shotgun. They had ditched the antiquated weapons stolen from the old fartsack in the shack near Chimayo with one exception: the four-barrel flintlock shotgun. Its hand-rotated barrels moved quickly and smoothly making it especially lethal at close range.

"I figgered you boys was just laying it on thick about this Fargo," Baylis remarked. "I didn't give a three-penny damn about him. But Katy Christ! He's already writ up in the papers. We done for his pard so now we got to do for him."

"How?" chimed in Hiram Steele. "I done my part. I bribed the hotel clerk and got his location, but Jed screwed the pooch and missed. Hell, it wasn't even Fargo in the window. So *how* we gonna get him?"

"How long is a piece of string?" Baylis replied irritably. "We'll just have to wait for the main chance."

"Waiting ain't a smart play," Steele persisted. "Not with a man like Fargo. You read in the paper how that old duffer we killed once saved Fargo's life. *He* sure's hell ain't waiting. What if he finds this place?"

"He don't know sic 'em about where we are. Anyhow, we ain't here to roost. Fargo don't put snow in *my* boots. I aim to carve him into a pile of tripes."

Baylis turned his eyes on Nearhood, who was busy cleaning his fingernails with a horseshoe nail. "Ray, ain't you got some rich cousin in Santa Fe?"

"Distant cousin. Frank Tutt. He owns the Gilded Cage. But he wouldn't piss in my ear if my brains was on fire. He's crooked as cat shit, like me, but he's one a them 'refined' fuckers that wears silk underdrawers and lifts his leg when he farts so it won't toot."

"Frank Tutt," Baylis repeated, a grin dividing his big, bluff, heavy-jowled face. "Ain't he the one's got that pretty Mexer hoor?"

"Rosita, yeah. Pretty? Mister, she could make a dead man come."

A smile divided Baylis' face. "Well, this might turn out mighty providential."

Nearhood looked confused. "That's too far north for me. You want to chew it a little finer?"

"Some Mex deputy was shootin' off his yap in the saloon about how Fargo and this Rosita was sniffing each other at the Sloan place and laying plans to play hide-the-sausage. Now, tell me, Ray, how would your cousin like that?"

"He'd piss blood, that's how. When we was kids, he beat me senseless for stealing one of his marbles."

"Wouldn't it just be easier," Hiram Steele suggested, "to stake out wherever this beaner whore lives and just shoot Fargo to rag tatters when he shows up? He's a helluva pussy hound and it won't be long before he taps that stuff. Prob'ly tonight."

"We'll plant him, all in good time," Baylis said. "But, boys, I been cogitating—we been playing the penny-ante game too long. *Let* Fargo prong her first. Then Ray goes to his cousin— us siding him, of course—and spills the beans. We offer to kill Fargo. Would your cousin likely go for that, Ray?"

"Likely. But what's your angle?"

Baylis hooked his thumbs into his shell belt. "Well, right off the top is the money—this Gilded Cage is packed with high rollers. Tutt can pay good, real good."

"Sure, why not?" Longstreet said. "We have to kill Fargo anyway, so why do it for free?"

"*Now* you're whistling," Baylis said. "It's called looking for the main chance."

Fargo slept until nine p.m., visions of the sun-haired Leora and the raven-haired Rosita dancing in his head like naked sugarplums. When he woke up, Wade was still snoring loud as a sawmill, his Colt Army lying beside his pillow. Fargo grinned. The kid was starting to understand the western frontier.

Fargo had insisted on a room with a *tronca* over the door, a solid bar of wood that fit into brackets on either side of the door. When he left, he woke up the sleepy soldier long enough for Wade to slip the bar back in place. Then Fargo ducked out of the hotel by a side entrance used by workers.

He stood in the shadow of the five-story building until his eyes had adjusted to night vision. Then he studied every potential ambush point carefully before he knocked the thong off the hammer of his Colt and walked up to Calle Linda.

This pretty treelined street was mostly nice homes and a few daytime businesses such as jewelry shops and dry goods stores. He opted for the middle of the cobblestone street, the heel of his palm resting on the butt of his Colt. Assassins were lurking somewhere, and it was Fargo's long habit to assume his next heartbeat could be his last if he didn't remain ever vigilant.

As he approached Avenida Mayor, Santa Fe's main street that included the Gilded Cage gambling house, the nighttime ruckus of a frontier boomtown assaulted his ears. Piano music, the tinny notes of hurdy-gurdies, celebration shots, raucous shouts and laughter—all of it formed a steady din.

Fargo spotted the alley Rosita had mentioned, a rutted mess just wide enough for a freight wagon. He already knew where the Gilded Cage was located, and he grinned when he saw a milk-glass lamp burning brightly on an upstairs window ledge. A scud of clouds swept in front of the moon, and Fargo made his move to the foot of the wooden stairs out back.

He suddenly froze in place, feeling pins and needles on the back of his neck. He thought he heard breathing coming from under the stairs. Fargo shucked out his barking iron and cocked it, slipping his finger inside the trigger guard. He squatted on his heels and took up the slack, waiting for violence to break the stillness.

"Lower your hammer, Trailsman," a familiar gravelly voice said. "Hell, I wouldn't murder a *living legend*. Half the skirts in America would be out to geld me."

Sheriff Hank Kinkaid stepped out from the dark shadows into the moonlight.

"You catch a lot of lawbreakers under those stairs?" Fargo asked.

"No, just a lot of damn fools. Fargo, you quiff-crazy idiot, I'll tell you straight from the shoulder. Rosita may be a mighty tempting woman, but she's death to the devil. You don't *even* want to cross Frank Tutt. His money and fancy duds don't signify—he's mean and low and spiteful, the brooding kind that holds a grudge until it hollers mama. And even though he ain't a killer himself, he hires it out."

"I know the type," Fargo replied matter-of-factly, "and I take special pleasure in topping their women. What's got me curious is—why are you bothering to warn me? You sweet on Rosita?"

"Fargo, an ugly cuss like me is sweet on *all* pretty gals. I'd give a purty just to see her naked. I mean that. I'm fifty years old and the only women I been with is soiled doves—ugly soiled doves. Even they don't get naked. They just hitch up their chemise so you can poke it in 'em. So I was kinda wondering . . . I mean . . ."

Kinkaid trailed off, suddenly ashamed. Fargo cocked his head in amazement.

"Sheriff, are you saying you want me to ask Rosita if you can have a whack at her when I'm—"

"Christ no, Fargo, you damn fool! She's a kept woman but she ain't no whore. No, I just want to see her naked. Just for a minute or two. Then I'll hightail it, my hand to God."

Fargo was both amazed and amused. And if Kinkaid was telling the truth, he also felt sorry for the old lawman. No man should go to his grave never having seen a gorgeous woman naked.

"Well, she might slap the shit out of me," Fargo finally replied. "Or she might even like the idea—she's a feisty little senyoreeter. C'mon up with me."

"Hold off a second," Kinkaid said gruffly. "Don't get the idea this cancels out anything I said yesterday about these damn killers. It ain't none of your mix."

"Yeah. Why'n't you set it to music?"

"Boy, I don't like that tone. And why are you and that toy soldier hanging around Santa Fe? You ain't a board walker."

"You should tell me, Kinkaid. After all, you're the jasper that ran to the newspapers so the killers will know I'm here. And you ask *me* for a favor like this one? I should tell you to go crap in your hat."

"That was dealing from the bottom of the deck," Kinkaid admitted, now following Fargo up the stairs. "I meant to scare you off. And it better have. So help me Hannah, Fargo, if you two jays go on a killing spree, my posse will dog you to the gates of hell."

"You'll have to ride farther," Fargo assured him. "I'm not one to be stopped by gates. Speaking of your posse, any progress yet?"

"Ain't seen hide nor hair of the gang. But they're close by. Sure as sun in the morning they're close by."

Fargo told himself that was for damn sure—close enough to send a slug into his hotel room. But he kept that incident dark from the sheriff.

Fargo rapped softly on the door of the landing, and it was answered almost immediately by a smiling Rosita. She wore only a sheer silk chemise, and the light from the sumptuous living quarters behind her outlined a slender, curving body.

"Fargo," she welcomed him in a voice made husky from anticipation, "I am on fire between my legs for—*ay!*"

She had just spotted the lawman almost hiding behind Fargo. He removed his hat and twirled it around nervously in his hands. Rosita made no effort to cover herself, however—Fargo took that as a good sign.

"You both came together?" she asked Fargo, dark eyes smoldering with suspicion.

"No," Fargo said, "I ran into the sheriff in the alley. But he has a favor to ask of you. Can we go inside? I feel like a target up here."

Girding his loins—for Fargo had already tasted the wrath of a pissed-off Mexican woman—he tactfully explained Kinkaid's strange, perverse request. To his surprise, she seemed almost flattered.

"I am proud of my naked beauty," she told the sheriff, making him grin like a butcher's dog. "And pleased that you wish to see me above other women. But only a brief look, *verdad?* And you must not come back next time saying now it must be a touch. Your favor is granted this one time only."

"Square deal," he promised. "Hell, Rosita, just looking at you in that dainty whatchacallit is worth ten trips to a cat-house."

Fargo had to agree. Like many Mexican women she had a full, jet-black bush of pubic hair and it pressed revealingly against the sheer fabric. Likewise her hard, heavy tits with their cocoa-colored nipples dinting the chemise. With a fast, sweeping gesture of her arms, she pulled the garment off and stood stark naked in the soft light of a parlor done mostly in red damask.

"Good god-*damn*," Kinkaid said in a voice just above a whisper.

"I'll second that," Fargo said, suddenly realizing just how

woman-hungry he was after the long ride from the Indian Territory. He abruptly sat down to hide his rock-hard erection—not from Rosita but from the sheriff.

Rosita did a slow twirl to show Kinkaid her taut, high-split ass and the sexy dimples at the base of her spine. Fargo hid a grin behind his hand when he saw Kinkaid self-consciously move his hat in front of his crotch.

"Damn, thank you much, Rosita," the badge-toter said suddenly, turning to let himself out. "I got something to take care of—right now."

Fargo laughed outright as soon as the door was shut. "*Querida*, thanks to you some poor whore will earn her two dollars tonight."

"What about you, tamer of wanton women?" she teased. "Are you aroused, too?"

It was a wide, solid wing chair, so Fargo didn't stand on formalities. He leaned back, opened his fly, and let his turgid manhood spring into view, so hard the glans was purple and his shaft twitched with each heartbeat.

"*Ay, Dios mio! Que largo eres!* Such a size on you I have seen only on stallions! *Los diario*s—how you say—the newspapers say nothing of this."

"Come try it on for size," Fargo invited. "You'll see it fits perfect."

She straddled his lap and grabbed his twitching pizzle, running a tight fist up and down its length and igniting a fiery pleasure that made Fargo pant like an overheated animal.

"*Muy duro*," she said in a rasping whisper. "So hard! And my fingers barely close around it! Fargo, *vamos a chingar.* Now we are going to do it, and you will make me explode, *verdad?*"

She bent his shaft to the perfect angle and slid forward onto it. She cried out and Fargo hissed in sudden pleasure as his probing length parted the snug velvet walls of her sex. He let the strong-willed beauty control their rhythm, more than content with her erotic style. For a few minutes, perhaps sensing he would climax too soon, she rode him slowly from base to tip, shooting galvanic tickles of pleasure through his shaft and groin.

Those luscious honeydews were mashed into his face and

Fargo worked both chamois-soft nipples with his lips, teeth, and tongue, fuel on fuel to the fire building inside her. Soon her pent-up lust had reached the pressure point, and Rosita ground harder and faster on his erection, becoming so carried away that Fargo had to grab her ass with both hands to keep her in the chair.

"*Ay!*" she cried. "Fargo, here it comes! *Ay! Ay, caramba!*"

Her last few plunges were so violent that the heavy chair tilted precariously on its back legs. But Fargo's equally forceful plunges as he drove forward into her brought the chair upright again as both peaked together, Fargo requiring nearly a dozen finishing thrusts to spend himself.

So powerful was their release that both went limp as rag dolls for countless minutes. When Fargo floated back to the surface of awareness, he was still inside Rosita and she was moving her hips in a pleasure rhythm.

"You never even went soft!" she marveled. "Truly you *are* a stallion! This one will be even better. Buck, stallion, buck!"

But before Fargo could even find his rhythm, heavy, rapid steps drummed nearby. "Rosita, you goddamn two-bit whore, I'll kill you *and* that worthless drifter!"

Rosita leaped off Fargo, grabbing for her chemise. "*Maldito!* It is Frank! Someone must have seen you come up!"

The steps pounded closer, more than one man. Fargo, hastily fastening his belt and scooping his gun belt off the floor, aimed for the door on the landing.

"No!" Rosita told him. "He will have a paid killer waiting to shoot you. Use the side window—there is a—how you say—lightning rod you can slide down."

But it was too late. An interior door banged open and two men charged into the front parlor. One, a Mexican dressed all in black and with a six-gun in hand, pivoted toward Fargo. The Trailsman tucked and rolled just as the gun barked, shattering a vase. A second shot thwapped into the floor inches from Fargo's head.

The Trailsman came up to a kneeling position with his Colt cocked. It leaped in his fist and a neat hole opened in the Mexican's forehead, followed a heartbeat later by a scarlet rope of blood. The man fell with a hard thud, his heels scratching the carpet a few times as his nervous system tried to deny the fact of death.

"Jesus Christ!" shouted a short, powerfully built man with his red hair combed in a high crest. "You screw my woman and then you murder my hired hand? Fargo, you just dug your own grave."

Fargo casually swung the Colt's muzzle onto Frank Tutt. "If that's the case, then why not plug you, too? I ain't no half-way man."

Tutt looked at the unblinking eye of the gun and swallowed hard. "I ain't heeled, Fargo. Everybody knows I carry no weapons. And I ain't a greasy tumbleweed like you—I'm one of the topkicks in this city."

Fargo laughed. "Yeah, you'll get jewels in paradise for that. You got no witness that I 'murdered' your lick-finger, and you know damn well that in the West there's no murder conviction if the bullet hole is in front."

Tutt did know that and he dropped the subject, turning to Rosita. "You vile slut. So my informants were right. Letting this shiftless no-'count bummer point your heels to the sky."

"As for your insults of me, Tutt," Fargo said almost amiably, "they've already cost you your life, but we'll ford that river later. As for Rosita here, much as I'd like to enjoy her favors, that's not what I'm here for."

"I s'pose you came for a revival meeting, and her dressed—*un*dressed—like that? I didn't just fall off the turnip wagon."

"I barged in on her. She was out at the Sloan place yesterday when the bodies were discovered. A good friend of mine up in Chimayo was killed by the same bunch that done for the Sloans. I aim to find them and kill them. I was just asking Rosita some questions."

Hitherto, Tutt's face had been a scornful twist. Now it settled into a thoughtful frown. "Yeah, I read about that today. And that would explain why Kinkaid came up with you."

Fargo realized he was being watched close. "These informants you mentioned? Who might they be?"

Tutt shook his head. "I'm a gambler, Fargo. I hold my cards close."

"If I find out you're feeding at the same trough as those

murderers, you're going over the mountains, Tutt. Ain't enough hired killers in hell to save you."

Gamblers were fond of hideout guns, so Fargo backed toward the door.

"Wait," Tutt said. "Just now you said you'd be killing me for insulting you tonight. Was that on the square?"

Fargo nodded. "My friends can insult me, but I brook no insults from the likes of you. You'll answer for it."

"Jesus Christ, Fargo! I came up here thinking you were poking my woman. Don't that entitle a man to some insults? The hell would you do?"

"I've never laid claim to a woman," Fargo replied, "and I don't worry about who tops them. But I take your point. A simple apology now will end it."

"Shit, how can you call me out when I never go heeled?"

Fargo lifted one shoulder. "I've beat men to death with my bare fists. There's always a way."

Tutt's eyes fell to Fargo's hands. The knuckles were indeed layered with old scar tissue.

"All right." He finally surrendered. "I apologize."

"Accepted. Now get out on that landing and call off your hired gun down in the alley. I'd hate to kill two of your job-bers in one night."

# 10

The morning sun was still a pink blush on the eastern horizon when Fargo and Wade McKenna rose and dressed, strapping on their gun belts. Fargo announced they'd be riding, so Wade donned a long gray duster to protect his civilian clothing.

"Why'n't you get hold of a bonnet, too?" Fargo roweled him. "You'll get more use out of it than from that derby hat."

They were among the first arrivals in the vast dining room decorated with miniature fruit trees in wooden tubs. Fargo stared in disbelief when their breakfast platters were delivered.

"God's garters! Almost seventy bits a night, and *this* is the chewin's they give us? Damn skinny folded-over pancakes? Where's the grits and potatoes and side meat?"

"These aren't pancakes, Mr. Fargo. They're called crepes. The French love them."

"Bully for the French. I like food I can sink my teeth into."

Fargo cut one of the crepes in half and forked a piece into his mouth.

"Mighty tasty at that," he admitted. "But it won't slake my appetite."

"Especially after last night, huh?" Wade prompted, casting a sly glance his way.

"I thought you were an officer and a gentleman? A gentleman neither asks nor tells about conquests unless they're on the battlefield."

"Ahh . . . that's hogwash. I had instructors at the Academy who bragged about their intrigues."

Fargo snorted. "Intrigues my sweet aunt. I damn near got my guts irrigated when Frank Tutt and one of his dirt-workers

71

busted in. I had to kill the gun thrower—he was determined to get my life over."

Wade's fork clattered to his plate. "Kill the . . . but how did Tutt know you were up there?"

"Now, see, that's a stumper. He said 'informants' told him—more than one."

Wade pulled at his chin. "And you're thinking it was the Butcher Boys?"

He used the name coined by a newspaper writer.

"I got no hand-to-God proof, kid. But it ciphers. We already know they're watching us like a cat on a rat—that bullet that flew into our room yesterday proves that. Say . . . here's your goddess, and in fine form."

Leora Padgett, her bodice flattered by a cut-velvet dress, her blond hair pulled into a tight chignon under a silk net, entered the dining room accompanied by her copper-haired friend Constance. Her father and another middle-aged man, both dressed in the attire of respectable merchants, followed the women in.

"I talked to the one named Constance for a few minutes last night," Wade reported. "It seems old man Padgett is in town for a few weeks to organize a caravan for the King's Highway. That other man is Constance's father. They're all from Albany."

Fargo grinned. "That copper-haired gal is what they call an operator—real forward. Why'n't you mount a campaign, trooper?"

Wade's mouth turned down at the corners in a frown. "I was thinking about it, but she only looks good from a distance. Up close you can see her buck teeth. She does like to talk, though, and she says Leora is 'captivated' by you."

Fargo already knew that. Even now she was playing peek-a-boo with him, and he liked it just fine. Her frowning father, however, shot daggers at the Trailsman with his eyes.

"His Nibs would like to buckshot my ass," Fargo said, tossing Mr. Padgett a snappy two-fingered salute.

But while women were always welcome diversions, he hadn't come to Santa Fe to divert himself.

"Jawboning over this weak coffee and French pancakes

won't get us anywhere," he announced, grabbing his hat off the table. "Let's go talk to Manuel at the feed stable."

Fargo deliberately chose the main entrance of the hotel as the two men headed outside.

"Keep your eyes peeled," he advised his young companion, "but don't be obvious about it. We know what at least one of the sewer rats looks like. And one is all we need."

No shots rang out, perhaps because the street was not yet busy—Santa Fe, unlike most American cities, was filled with late risers.

As they strolled along the boardwalk, Fargo noticed a small, ugly man on the opposite side of the street. He appeared to be gazing at goods in the various shop windows, but his seedy, unwashed appearance and furtive manner didn't match a casual shopper on fashionable Calle Linda.

"Left flank at the next street," Fargo told Wade. "I think that mudsill across the street is salting our tails. He fits the description that room clerk gave us."

The two men turned suddenly and Fargo pulled Wade into a narrow alley. Less than a minute later the mysterious man hurried past the alley and Fargo collared him, jerking him in with them. He snatched the man's Colt Navy from its canvas holster and tossed it ten feet away.

"A pockmarked face," Fargo said grimly. "Wade, meet one of the Butcher Boys."

"Mister, you're mighty mistaken. I'm just a field hand down on his luck."

Fargo stared into those tiny piglike eyes and remembered what Corey had looked like when he found him. He let go of the man's shirt just long enough to slam him with a quick one-two punch followed by a hard jab to the stomach that doubled the man over.

"Are you the cutter?" Fargo said with quiet menace. "Or do all four of you take turns?"

Fargo gave the kneeling man enough time to get his breath back. "*Give*, you crater-faced sheep humper, or I'll feed your liver to your asshole. Where's your gang roosting?"

Fargo drew one leg back to fetch the "field hand" a good kick in the teeth.

"Fargo!" an authoritative voice bellowed from the alley entrance. "Down off your hind legs! What's all the catarumpus?"

Sheriff Kinkaid moved into the alley, repeater in hand.

"This is one of the Butcher Boys," Fargo said. "He tried to shoot Wade yesterday and he's following us today, hoping to back-shoot us."

"In a pig's ass," the rodentlike man snarled, acting tough now that the law was here. "I was just out stretching my legs and these two sonsabitches waylaid me."

"You got proof on this hombre?" Kinkaid demanded of Fargo. "Proof that will back an arrest warrant and nail his ass in court?"

Fargo stewed in bitter frustration. This man fit the description the clerk had given, all right. And clearly he was shadowing him and Wade. But he hadn't actually seen Crater Face shoot through that hotel window, nor could he actually prove the man was following them.

"I got no hand-to-God proof," he finally admitted. "But—"

"Yeah, I thought so. You," he said to the man, "pick up your hat and dust."

"Ain't you gonna arrest these two—"

"How do I know you didn't start the ruckus? I don't like the look of you. Dust your hocks before I arrest you as a vagrant."

The man scuttled away. Kinkaid turned to Fargo. "I knew you'd lord it around just on account you done me that little favor last night with Rosita."

Fargo shook his head. "Damn it, Sheriff, that's one of the men who killed and butchered out the Sloan family and Corey Webster."

"And two soldiers," Wade chimed in.

"It don't matter, you two ain't wearing a badge. Well, I see both of you got your minds set on mixing into this. I won't brook defiance, do you hear me? I don't care a frog's fat ass about the newspaper hokum, Fargo. This is *my* town, and no man is above the law."

"Except for the rich bastards," Fargo corrected him. "Like Frank Tutt."

Kinkaid's florid face turned even redder and his dark eyes snapped sparks. "I can't change that, Fargo, no man can. The Quality set their own rules everywhere."

"Not in my book, Kinkaid. I recognize only two classes: the Quality and the Equality. Ain't that why we popped the British over?"

Kinkaid was silent for a long moment. "Well . . . you've got a point and I'm caught upon it, I reckon. But we ain't talking about quality with this Butcher Boys gang. Just let me handle it. I've already sworn in deputies, and all four of those mad dogs will dance on air."

Kinkaid's tired, weather-cracked face softened a bit. "I hear they buried one of Tutt's gunmen today."

"Is that a loss to the community?"

Kinkaid snorted. "If you call losing a case of the runny shits a loss. I checked—the bullet hole was in the front. I got no dicker with self-defense, Fargo. Just remember what I told you and this little piss-squirt pard of yours. You don't have to be with me, Fargo. But if I find out you're agin us, you'll hang with the others."

"I won't stand in your way," Fargo promised.

But neither, he promised himself, would he stand aside.

Fargo searched everywhere for the shifty spy, but he had vamoosed without a trace. The two men walked to the livery at the southern outskirts of town without incident.

"Is that sheriff honest?" Wade asked along the way.

"Middling, or so I'm told. But like you just saw, he's plumb bullheaded when he gets his dander up."

"You think he'd really hang us for interfering in this Butcher Boys deal?"

"Naw. But he's a cantankerous son of a bitch and as territorial as a she-grizz with cubs. He *would* jug us, though, and that takes us out of the hunt. I've never shot an honest sheriff yet, and I won't start with him. We're standing on dynamite and we best step real careful."

They found their horses in the paddock, the Ovaro enjoying a good roll in the dirt.

The young mozo, Benito, was busy repairing a broken singletree. At Fargo's request, he ran to fetch Manuel.

"**Been** any suspicious characters asking you anything?" Fargo said. "About us or our horses?"

Manuel took off his hat to swipe at flies. "No one. And if they did I would tell them nothing. Your horses are safe here—at night there are dogs sleeping near the stalls and the paddock."

Fargo nodded. "I know. That's why I came here. Tell me, Manuel—there must be plenty of robbers' roosts in this area. Can you think of any that are fairly close to town? Close enough that men could come and go without too much riding time?"

The aging man's seamed brown face set itself in thoughtful concentration. "There are a few, I think: Los Hornos to the southwest; Twin Forks to the north; and Duro Canyon due west."

"Which one is closest to Santa Fe?"

"*Pues*, Duro Canyon is surely the farthest—perhaps ten miles. The other two are perhaps the same distance, about three miles."

Fargo mulled this. "Would you say that one has any advantages over the other—advantages for outlaws, I mean."

"Twin Forks is better hidden, I think. Farther off the trail. There is an old miner's shack there and the place is—how you say—surrounded by a shallow, rocky basin. *Por eso*, it is more difficult to sneak up on anyone hiding there."

"How do we find it?"

"Ride due north out of town and watch for a lightning-split cottonwood—this is how the place got its name. Turn right at this tree and ride another half mile until you reach the basin. You will see the shack from the tree cover. But *ten cuidado*—anyone in the shack has a perfect view in all directions."

"'Preciate the hell right out of it, Manuel," Fargo told him, pressing a gold dollar into his hand.

"Might be a wild-goose chase," Wade remarked as they retrieved their tack and rigged their mounts.

"I've chased plenty of wild geese in my life," Fargo assured him. "When you're riding after owlhoots, you'll seldom get a map to their hideout."

The Ovaro nuzzled Fargo's shoulder as he slid the bridle

on, taking the bit easily and eager to stretch out the kinks. Both men carefully inspected cinches, latigos, and stirrups before forking leather and reining their mounts north. They passed through town at a trot, then opened their mounts up to a lope.

Fargo spotted the split cottonwood first.

"Here's the turnoff," he told Wade, reining in. "Check your loads."

The tree cover was thick and they advanced at a walk, Fargo's eyes narrowed as they watched for a sentry outpost. But they reached the edge of the rocky basin without incident. The miner's shack, a tumbledown structure of weather-rotted planks, stood in the center of the basin. A trio of horses were hobbled behind it.

"Only three mounts," Wade remarked.

"Yeah, but Crater Face might still be hiding in town," Fargo pointed out.

The two men were still hidden in the trees. Fargo sized up the situation with the eye of a trained scout who knew how best to use terrain.

"Here's the way of it. There's just enough ground cover, if we move low and slow, to get about halfway to that shack. After that it's nothing but small rocks that wouldn't conceal a woodchuck. If we try to sneak up the rest of the way, they'll pick us off like lice from a blanket."

"You mean, we should just rush them the rest of the way?"

Fargo shook his head. "We ain't the cavalry here, son. Forget West Point. When we were in Corey's shack, I noticed his favorite weapon was missing: a four-barrel shotgun. It's an old flintlock, but it shoots fast and that double-aught buckshot would blow us to chair stuffings."

"Wait until dark?"

"That's a long ways off. I got a better plan: We bluff them into surrendering. Most outlaws are cowards and if they think they're outgunned by a posse, they'll usually show the white feather. Hell, a good number of them manage to escape before they get to jail—why not play the smart odds?"

"All that makes sense," Wade agreed. "But we're not a posse."

"No, but they don't know that. I was hoping to avoid a

shooting affray, but we have to play the cards we're dealt. Now listen, you're going to have to bloody your elbows and knees to do this. We both spread out as we crawl. When you hear my Henry open up, blast that shack with all seven rounds from your carbine. Those .56 slugs will rattle them good. Then immediately switch to your sidearm and empty the wheel. When it's empty, reload both weapons quicker than scat. But keep your head down. Clear on the plan?"

The lieutenant looked nervous but gamely nodded. "Don't worry about me. There's a plaque over the door of the mess hall at the Point: 'Gentlemen, you must exert yourselves.' Only a bullet will stop me."

Fargo grinned. "That plaque sounds jim-dandy to me. Now let's take it off the wall and put it into the fight."

# 11

They hobbled their horses foreleg to rear with strips of raw-hide. Both men slid their rifles from the scabbards. Fargo was relying on the Henry's 16-shot magazine to pull this off, but he had to envy Wade's carbine for its size and lightness—low-crawling with a weapon as long as a Henry was no easy feat.

As the morning sun heated up they began moving out over the hard, flinty terrain. Fargo had called it right: Flakes of flint and obsidian permeated the dirt and tore into their elbows and knees. They could rise only a few inches because of the low cover that made progress agonizingly slow.

"Get your butt down, shavetail," Fargo called over to Wade in a low but commanding voice. "There's a window in the front of that shack, and I see a face watching this approach."

It was late in the forenoon now, and rivulets of sweat poured down from Fargo's thick brown hair, stinging his eyes. Worse, gnats kept swarming his face. Eventually, though, both men, now separated by about fifty feet, reached the periphery of the safe cover. The shack sat about seventy-five yards ahead.

Fargo welcomed the prospect of raw action to break up the tedium of that long crawl. He jacked a round into the Henry's breech and laid a bead on the door of the shack. The rifle bucked into his shoulder as Fargo opened the ball.

He didn't let up, levering and firing, levering and firing, shell casings clattering into the rocks. He could hear Wade's Spencer cracking rapidly, the big slugs knocking chunks of wood off the shack. He expected the outlaws to cover down, but at least two of them had spotted their powder smoke and were laying down return fire.

"Keep rolling to new positions, Wade!" he sang out. "Don't give 'em a bead!"

A ricochet whanged past Fargo's ear so close the wind from it tickled him. Another near miss threw rock chips into his face, but Fargo worked the Henry's mechanism with machine precision. The quieter pops from Wade's position told him the soldier had switched to his short gun. Fargo emptied the Henry's magazine and followed suit with his Colt.

By now the wall of lead tearing into the shack had quelled all return fire. As Fargo slipped his spare cylinder into the Colt he shouted out, "Hallo, the shack! This is a U.S. marshal's posse and we've got a net around you! Toss out your shooters and come out with your hands on your head! If you don't, we'll shoot you to trap bait!"

Fargo heard the men arguing among themselves. A voice he thought he recognized rose in volume above the rest. "We're in one world of shit, chappies! Me, I'll take my chances any day in a territorial court over bucking a posse."

A moment later the same voice called out, "All right, law dogs, hold your fire! We're comin' out!"

Rifles and handguns arced out through the door and skittered on the rocks. Three men marched out single file, hands on their heads.

"Shit, piss, and corruption," Fargo swore in an angry voice.

Wade had edged closer to Fargo's position and heard the cursing. "What's wrong?" he demanded.

"We got the wrong bunch," Fargo said. "See that hombre with the red bandanna and the hawk nose? That's Ace Ludlow. My trail has crossed his for years."

"They look like desperadoes to me."

"Ace is bad medicine, all right, but nobody ever marked him down for a killer. Him and those two sidewinders with him are hard-bitten bastards who 'druther risk getting shot to doing honest work. But compared to the Butcher Boys, they're small potatoes."

Fargo stood up, Colt trained on the trio. "Hey, Ace. How they hanging?"

"Pretty high and tight right now, Marshal. We—shit! Is that you, Skye Fargo?"

"It ain't Queen Victoria."

"You ain't no goddamn law. Hell, I heard you beat the

dog shit outta some star-packer in Sacramento and left town at a two-twenty clip."

"I don't mind being arrested," Fargo explained. "But not for whoring on Sunday. Hell, I was keeping rhythm to the church bells."

"This pup siding him," the man closest to Ace remarked, "looks fresh out of short pants. What the hell kind of play is this?"

"That pup is a dead aim," Fargo warned. "You two keep edging toward them weapons, you'll die of surprise."

"Fargo ain't bluffing, boys," Ace warned. Then he added, "But why the hell are you arresting us? You ain't no law."

"I'm not arresting you," Fargo admitted. "It's what you might call a case of mistaken identity."

"But you said they're outlaws," Wade protested. "One of us can hold them under citizen's arrest while the other rides for Sheriff Kin—oh!"

Fargo laughed when the kid realized the bind they were in. Kinkaid had just lectured them on the dangers of usurping his authority.

"What are you boys holed up here for?" Fargo asked.

Ace lifted a shoulder. "Ahh, you know how it goes. We robbed a stagecoach out in Arizona not realizing some big-bug politician was on board. We had to skedaddle. You said you ain't arresting us, Fargo, and I happen to know that your word is your bond. But are you going to turn us in?"

Fargo had no plans to assist Kinkaid, especially after all his damn lecturing earlier allowed Crater Face to escape. But neither was he happy about letting these three owlhoots ply their trade around Santa Fe.

When Fargo didn't answer right away, Ace added, "You owe us one, Fargo. 'Member when them Cheyenne Dog Soldiers had you trapped in that gulch near the Rosebud? You run out of ammo and them featherheads was about to lift your dander, but me and the boys choused them off."

"You did," Fargo conceded, "but then you robbed me of every cent I had."

"So? We left your horse, your weapons, and even gave you loads for your short gun. We're thieves, Fargo, but we got us a code."

"When a man's right, he's right," Fargo said. "I won't mention you're here to anybody. But if I learn of you three jays pulling a heist around here, I'll have to put the law on your scent."

Ace grinned. "Square deal. Who was you expecting when you shot that shack to kindling?"

Ace's gang had been holed up, so Fargo told them about the Butcher Boys and asked if they had seen them.

"Christ no," Ace replied, his face pale. "Butchered out the Sloan women? Why, hell, we stopped there to water our horses and them two pretty ladies fed us a good meal. We didn't have the heart to rob them."

"Mighty white of you," Wade chimed in sarcastically.

"Wipe off your chin, squirt," one of Ace's men snapped.

"Listen, Fargo," Ace said, "you must have seen that lightning-split tree beside the trail. If we find out anything, I'll leave you a note there. I won't rat out a fellow thief, but any sick-brained son of a bitch who butchers out old men and decent women needs to be cut down for the rabid cur he is. Square deal?"

Fargo nodded once. "Square deal. But leave your weapons where they are until me and the lieutenant here clear this basin. I know you won't shoot us, but you will lighten our wallets."

Ace laughed. "Hell yes, that's what we do."

When the two men had reversed their dust toward Santa Fe, Wade broke his brooding silence.

"I know that Ludlow fellow saved your life, Mr. Fargo. But, hell, he also robbed you. And he admits to robbing stagecoaches. I think we let those three off too light."

"I can see your side of it," Fargo said. "In its way, soldiering is a law-and-order job. But we've already heard the riot act from Kinkaid twice now."

"I'm not talking about arresting them. Just reporting their whereabouts to him."

Fargo sighed as if he were trying to explain calligraphy to a mule. "And what reason would we give old bullheaded Hank for nosing around known robbers' roosts? Tell him we were just out for a picnic?"

"Well, I s'pose—"

"Suppose a cat's tail, you young fool. He'd know damn good and well we were out gunning for the Butcher Boys. And I wouldn't put it past him to toss us in the pokey until we finally come to Jesus."

"Yeah, I take your drift. And we could hardly find the butchers from a jail cell."

"Now you're whistling. Besides all that, I wouldn't turn Ace's bunch in anyway. I believe in live and let live. If he was a killer or rapist, sure—I'd tag him myself. But those three aren't much different from tax collectors."

Fargo felt a keen disappointment. He had bloodied knees and elbows, expended valuable ammunition, in a wasted fight. But he kept his eyes in vigilant motion, knowing his mistake didn't mean the gang couldn't be lurking nearby. He studied the shadows behind every stand of scrub oak or jack pine, every tumble of boulders. Mountains loomed on their left, but the terrain immediately around them was low hills cut with ravines.

"Why the hell you keep forcing that sorrel's head up?" he demanded, watching Wade repeatedly tug the reins up.

"Why, so he can see where he's going, I reckon."

"Blast West Point," Fargo muttered. "Soldier, my stallion's doing the same thing. All horses nose the ground in unfamiliar country—they're nervous by nature and sniffing the ground helps to settle them down. Besides, a horse's nose is sensitive to vibrations—they can 'hear' with it pressed into the dirt."

"That's in my notebook," the shavetail said. "And thanks. This is why I wanted to ride with you, Mr. Fargo."

"You may come to regret that before this deal is over. This bunch we're up against now are some of the sickest hard cases I've ever known of."

"Speaking of them . . . are we gonna try another roost today?"

Fargo knuckled his hat up and glanced up at the sun. "Still plenty of light left yet. Let's try this place called Los Hornos. Manuel said it's southwest of town off the old freight road."

The two men rode back through Santa Fe, the place much more bustling than when they'd left earlier. Pedro Valdez, Kinkaid's deputy, leaned lazily in front of the sheriff's office, watching the street. He met Fargo's eyes and touched the brim of his straw Sonora hat. Fargo nodded back.

"I don't know about him," Fargo remarked to Wade. "These quiet Mexicans are hard to read. They know how to hold their cards close."

"Surely you don't think he's somehow protecting the Butcher Boys? Hell, he saw what they did to the Sloan ladies, and he looked pretty sick about it."

"Oh, I think that was genuine, all right. Kinkaid wouldn't hire a deputy who was a cold-blooded killer. But I got a hunch that Frank Tutt may somehow be in touch with them—recall those 'informants' I told you about him mentioning? And Tutt has enough scratch to keep a lawman in his hip pocket, too."

"And maybe even a soldier?" Wade asked.

Fargo's head swiveled toward the young officer. "Well, the lad's a quick study. Major Bruce Harding does seem to live well above his pay grade—but that could be kickbacks from his gunsmith brother."

They followed the old freight road at a lope for the first couple of miles, then reined in to a trot to search for the elusive trail Manuel mentioned. Fargo's hawk eyes spotted it just past a dogleg bend in the road, so overgrown with weeds and creosote it was barely discernible.

"They might have a picket guard out," Fargo said as he gigged the Ovaro forward into the shadowed lane. "And Manuel says there's several little rock gullies to cross before we'll see the old Pueblo village. Keep your eyes to all sides."

Fifteen minutes of slow riding brought them to the end of the trail and the beginning of the first gully.

"I don't like it," Fargo decided after a quick reconnoiter. "Even at a walk, our shod horses are going to make a clatter on all those rocks. I've got a shoeing hammer, but if we pull our mounts' shoes we'll be useless for a chase. Since we won't have to crawl in this time, let's just hobble our horses here in the thickets. They'll be well protected."

Fargo slid his Henry from its saddle boot and thought about that lead they'd expended earlier. "How you set for loads, kid?"

"Twelve for my sidearm, only five for my carbine."

"Mm. I've got nine for my Henry and only six for my short

iron. Well, that's over thirty rounds between us, and you're a dead aim. This time, though, we don't try to smoke them out with that posse bluff. We save our lead for killing. Assuming they're even here, and we *are* going to assume that."

Each man taking opposite sides, they crossed the first small gully at a crouch. Fargo took heart in the fact that cover was sparse above them and any guard would have trouble hiding. The second gully started after only a hundred feet or so of sparse ground cover. Fargo gave Wade the high sign to halt and reconnoiter carefully. When they had studied the terrain minutely, they moved quickly forward again.

This time they moved at a quick trot and reached the last gully in a few minutes. Now Fargo could spot a few of the mud ovens that gave the place its name. Both men pressed as close to the walls of the gully as possible and moved forward in slow increments, Fargo always mindful that it was movement, not shape that caught an enemy's attention.

Halfway into the gully he spotted the crude shelter made of old wagon wood and canvas, leaning precariously to one side. There were no horses in sight, but this bunch, Fargo reminded himself, were in far more hot water than Ace's—meaning they might have been careful to tether their mounts somewhere in the pine trees behind the old Pueblo village.

Thinking that, he signaled Wade to join him after they debouched from the gully and reached a line of hawthorn bushes.

"You wait here," Fargo told him. "*Don't* break cover. I'm searching those trees straight ahead to see if they hid their mounts."

"Seems awful quiet," Wade said doubtfully. "And four men would go stir crazy in a little hovel like that. Seems like they'd hang around outside during the day."

"Yeah, it's hardly bigger than a packing crate, and it's hot enough outside to peel a rattler. But it's likely not all four are here at once—if any of them are. Anyhow, when I come back out of those trees I'm sneaking up on that shelter. That's when you take off and come up on this side. Leapfrog using those ovens and those boulders and bushes scattered around. Christ sakes, stay out of the open."

Relying on pine trees and scrub bushes, Fargo angled off

to the south of the dwelling and into the small pine woods. A quick search showed nothing, not even old droppings. Making sure Wade saw him he held his Henry at a high port and sprinted toward the shelter. When both men were in place, he edged around cautiously to the front. There was no door, just a wide-open front, and a quick glance showed they had drawn another low card.

Fargo tasted the bitter bile of disappointment. "Shit. Unlike Ace and his pards, this bunch was smart enough to rabbit."

"You sure they were ever here?"

Fargo nodded toward the ground. "Four horses were hobbled out here. And they just lit out today—some of these droppings are fresh."

Wade cast a nervous glance back toward the gullies. "Maybe they didn't light out. Maybe they'll be back."

"Could be, but I'm thinking no. A roost this well known is all right for a night or two while outlaws make more permanent plans. But these four are the scourge of the territory right now. They can't breathe easy here."

Fargo nodded toward the shelter. "And if they were coming back, they'd be likely to leave something behind—owlhoots are lazy sons of bitches who like to travel light. There's no food or water even—just old rusted cans."

"There's still this Duro Canyon to the west," Wade reminded him.

"Yeah, it's worth checking. But I think we'll just be washing bricks."

"Well, where do you think they'd go?"

Fargo shook his head. "Criminals are lazy as hell, and usually stupid. But they're cunning when it comes to throwing men off their trail. If they head south, which is the easiest riding, there's Rio Ranchos, Madrid, or Albuquerque. But all those places are just flyspecks on a map. Taos, to the northeast, is a little bigger, but four strangers riding in would be under close watch by Sheriff Buck Munro—one lawman who knows his hay foot from his straw foot."

"Well then, what's your best guess where they'll go?"

"You want the straight, soldier? Since outlaws are generally lazy and have poor trail craft, by nature they prefer cities—the bigger the better. And Santa Fe is the biggest city for hundreds of miles around."

The kid's jaw slacked open. "You think they'd hole up here after what they did to the Sloan ladies?"

Fargo nodded. "They need money to get any great distance, and nobody knows what they look like—except us, and we've only seen one. Since Sheriff Kinkaid won't believe us, even that crater-faced rodent is in the clear."

Wade thought about it, swiping sweat out of his eyes. "I guess you're right. Especially if they don't hang around together as a group of four."

Fargo was about to nod when something inside the crude shelter caught his eye—an object wrapped in cheesecloth and placed on top a rusted can, as if meant to capture notice. He reached inside, brought it out into the sunlight, and unwrapped it.

"God-in-whirlwinds!" Wade exclaimed, going pale as alkali dust.

Fargo stared, forcing himself not to drop it in disgust.

"When Corey Webster was younger," he finally managed to say, "he fought in the Blackfeet Indian Wars. The state of Illinois gave him a solid gold ring for his good service."

Fargo pointed to a wide white line around the severed ring finger. "The Butcher Boys couldn't get that ring off, so they just took the whole finger and got it later. They wanted me to find this."

Wade noticed a new glint of hard mettle in Fargo's eyes. "Hank Kinkaid can go piss up a rope, soldier blue. Those four maggots are mine."

A deadly calm had settled over the Trailsman—like the calm before a roaring, tumultuous storm. "Well, we best make tracks," he told his companion, "if we expect to make Santa Fe by sundown."

# 12

Santa Fe was a nocturnal city, and it was coming to bustling life now as the sun, a giant copper coin balanced on purple mountain peaks to the west, gave way to grainy twilight. The boardwalks were crowded with hawkers, lamplighters, and touts—young men who solicited business for saloons, gambling halls, and hotels.

In this pied flow of humanity, no one paid any attention to the two men who made an odd pair as they hugged the apron of shadows near the buildings. One was a barrel-chested mountain of a man with a broad, blunt-featured face. The other, skinny as a rail and nearly a foot shorter, wore a new floppy-brimmed hat that left much of his face in shadow.

"Hiram, for Christ sakes stop looking over your shoulder," Baylis Ulrick snapped. "If Fargo is out there watching the streets, you'll stand out like a Kansas City fire engine."

"Easy for you to say. *You* didn't have your nuts knocked up into your throat by that son of a bitch. He's strong as horseradish. I still say we should dust out of New Mexico Territory."

"He's a first-rate tracker, remember? You can't run from a man like him—not if you ever hope to sleep in peace. For us it's now root hog or die."

Steele pulled his new hat lower. "Whose fault is that? You're the one who sliced up his old pard into chitterlings. And then to top it off, you go and leave that damn finger for salt in the wound. Hell *yes* he'll track us down."

"Your big problem, Hiram, is you ain't got the mentality to take on a man like Fargo. Of course finding that finger will make him ireful—and ireful men get stupid and make mistakes. That's why I done it."

"Maybe you're right. And it *is* crowded in this town."

"That's the gait, bo. I told all three of you boys, we can keep Fargo flummoxed best by staying right here. Half the jaspers in this city are using summer names, and the flow of strangers in and out never lets up. And if we play your rich cousin right, we can douse Fargo's light, leave in style on a stagecoach and hole up in San Francisco."

The two men were heading down the main street toward Frank Tutt's Gilded Cage gambling house. Earlier they had used money stolen from the Sloan family to rent a lean-to room jutting off the back of Paddy's tavern. But by day the men now planned to pair off—Jed Longstreet and Ray Nearhood would not be seen with Ulrick and Steele, a key part of Ulrick's plan for dealing with Tutt, and eventually, Fargo.

"Yeah, old long shanks will get his comeuppance soon enough," Ulrick vowed. "But I admit it was a mistake to have you dog his trail 'steada Ray or Jed. Now he's seen your pan, but we need you to help palaver with your cousin Frank. That hat and them new duds should help some. Get you a bath and a shave, too. 'Course, can't nobody do nothing 'bout them pockmarks on your face. But plenty of men got smallpox scars."

"Ain't just me. We got to do for that bastard before he sees you and the others."

"Jesus Christ, Mildred, quitcher whining. We have to *profit* from the killing, too, and that means getting your cousin Frank into the mix deeper. That hunnert dollars he gave us for telling him Fargo was bulling his Mexer whore is pee doodles. But what you found in Tutt's place today—now *that's* medicine."

"Yeah," Hiram said, "he'll shit bricks when we tell him. But I'm thinkin' that's a queer deal about Rosita. I knew Frank's hired guns would never manage to kill Fargo, but it's common knowledge that any woman of Frank's who puts the horns on him ends up floating in the Rio Grande. But I spotted Rosita today with nary a mark on her."

"Them Mexican bitches could sell dynamite to a Quaker," Baylis said. "Either her or Fargo lied their way out of it. Or maybe your cousin is just scared spitless of the man. If that's the problem, then me and you are going to have to put blood in Cousin Frank's eyes."

Skye Fargo's eyes scoured the blue-black twilight as he and Wade McKenna thumped along the boardwalk from the livery to the heart of town. A number of hard cases, lounging negligently against posts and buildings, studied them from lidded eyes. He surprised a number of them by boldly walking up to them and tossing their hats aside to study their faces.

"The hell's biting at you, mister?" one of them demanded. But the moment he glimpsed Fargo's granite-carved features and implacable eyes, his hand left the butt of his six-gun. "Forget I asked," he added.

Fargo picked up his hat, knocked the dust off it, and clapped it on his head. "My mistake, old son."

Wade, like Fargo, studied every face they passed. "We only saw the one," he mused aloud, "but if you're right, they're out there somewhere. And they know what we look like."

"Thanks for reminding me," Fargo said. "There's a gun shop up ahead that keeps late hours. These shooters ain't much use without ammo, and we're both running short."

Fargo bought a hundred-count box of two-hundred-fifty-grain cartridges for his Colt and two boxes of four-hundred-fifty-grain bullets for his Henry. He added a box of wiping patches and a small can of gun oil, planking gold and earning an ear-to-ear smile from the proprietor. But when Wade presented his military chit, the man looked at him asquint.

"Boy, are you certain you're a soldier? Your peach fuzz I'm willing to overlook—I've seen troopers that look fresh-dragged from the tit. But that derby hat . . . son, you look like them scrubbed angels that hold the money box for temperance biddies."

Wade flushed to his earlobes, Fargo snickered, and the gunsmith folded his hands in mock prayer.

"It's all right," Fargo vouched for him. "His mother knows he's out."

Back on the boardwalk all Wade said was, "I'm getting shut of this damn hat."

"In an emergency," Fargo suggested, "you could water a gopher from it."

They strolled into the lobby of the Dorsey House and

Fargo's mood suddenly notched itself higher: Leora Padgett was seated by herself at a writing desk in the lobby, leafing through an issue of *Godey's Lady's Book*. Her golden tresses were fastened on both sides of her head with horn combs but tumbled down her back in a spun-gold waterfall. And Fargo gratefully noted the lobby was mostly empty except for a few older guests playing dominoes or checkers.

"See you later, Lieutenant McKenna," Fargo said pointedly when the soldier stuck to his side. Wade angled obliquely off.

"Did I keep you waiting long?" Fargo greeted her, his tone intended to get a rise out of her. He succeeded: For a moment he watched an angry vein pulse over her temple.

Those China blue eyes probed him, direct as searchlights. "Well, if it isn't the rough frontier specimen who wishes he could paint me." She surprised him pleasantly, however, by adding, "And I suppose you specialize in nudes?"

"Without your clothes on, I'd have less to paint, now wouldn't I?"

"That's a matter of perspective, no pun," she replied, giving him an up-and-under look Fargo could feel in his hip pocket. "Pardon my vanity, Mr. Fargo, but I'd say you'd have more to paint—much more."

Fargo's eyes slanted down from her finely sculpted face to the ample bosom of her white, flounce-bottom gown.

"I thought eyes were windows to the *soul*," she barbed after his silence grew noticeable.

"You can't hang a man for his thoughts."

"Nor a woman, I hope."

Fargo liked the direction this trail was taking. "Miss Padgett, out west you can't hang a woman for anything."

"Well! That leaves her a great deal of . . . latitude in her behavior."

"Which leads me to wonder—do you only undress for painters?"

"I bathe—if that word is in your vocabulary?"

"Oh, I'm town-broke—just barely. I s'pose I am a mite dusty right now, though."

"Yes, and frankly, it's quite becoming on you. In fact, I find you very . . . stimulating."

Fargo figured if he became any more "stimulated" he was

**91**

going to draw stares. "It appears to me that daddy's little filly has a very long tether."

He had struck a sour note, and a petulant frown disturbed her face. "My father doesn't like you. To him you're a worthless bummer."

"Well, old pater is right on that. I'd say there's an enterprising young buck back in Albany he wants you to marry."

"Yes, and likely I *will* marry him and ruin my figure by having babies. But what goes on way out here in Santa Fe is my little secret. Stored in the locket of my memory forever."

"Well, now, that rings right. But you have to *make* a memory before you can store it."

She nodded, her tone becoming more intimate. "Then let's make one. A good one. We can—"

"Leora!"

The moment Fargo recognized Henry Padgett's pissed-off voice he was tempted to shoot the man for rotten timing.

"Fargo," the merchant fumed as he strode briskly across the marble floor, closing in like an angry wolverine, "I asked you to leave my daughter alone. She's an innocent young girl and she wants none of your corrupting influence."

Leora's eyes met Fargo's for a heartbeat, and both struggled not to laugh. But Fargo was quite tolerant of abuse from certain men, and angry fathers fell into that category.

"She's quite innocent, Mr. Padgett, you're right. I was merely discussing famous works of art with her."

"My sweet aunt. Name one famous painting, Mr. Fargo."

"I will, Mr. Padgett, as soon as you tell me what it means when a horse's ears are cropped."

"I haven't the foggiest notion."

"I guess we all know what we need to," Fargo said as he headed toward the stairs. And he threw back over his shoulder: "My favorite painting is *L'Allegro* by Charles West Cope."

From the dizzying spiral staircase he cast a glance toward father and daughter. Henry Padgett looked as if he'd just heard a dog talk; Leora stared up at the crop-bearded, buckskin-clad frontiersman with new wonder and respect. Fargo had all he could do to keep from laughing outright—a copy of Cope's painting hung over his bed in the hotel room, the first time in his life he'd ever seen it.

She's going to climb all over me now, Fargo thought. Every man should dabble in culture.

Frank Tutt lifted the chimney from a coal-oil lamp and lit the wick with a sulfur match. Light splashed the rose-patterned carpet and pushed shadows back into the corners of his private office at the rear of the Gilded Cage. He took a seat behind his big oak desk and impatiently waved his visitors into a pair of cushioned chairs.

"Hiram, have you been grazing locoweed?" he demanded of his cousin. "I told you last time you came to stay away from here. This isn't a saloon for drifters and shit-heels, it's a high-class gambling establishment. Christ, the mayor is out front right now with several prominent merchants."

Hiram Steele balanced his new hat on his knee and smirked like a man who knows a mighty potent secret. "Say, Cuz, are you ashamed of your own kin?"

Tutt ignored him, casting a wary and curious glance at the big man with him. "Who's this?"

"Just call me John Doe this summer," Baylis Ulrick replied. "Drifter and shit-heel. Tell me something, Frank boy—how do you get that red hair of yours up in a rooster crest like that? If you didn't have such a good set of shoulders on you, I'd call you a gal-boy."

Too late, Tutt realized he should have taken one of his shootists into the office with him. But Fargo had left him one man short when he drilled Lenny, and another was now guarding the rear steps leading to Tutt's living quarters.

Impatiently, Tutt slipped three fingers into the fob pocket of his vest and slid out a gold-cased watch, sliding back the cover with his thumb. "Time is money to a busy man like me. If you two have a point, feel free to make it."

"No need to slip your traces," Hiram said. "We ain't in such an all-fired hurry as you, Cuz."

"Men of few means seldom are. You were always a wastrel, Hiram." Tutt averted his eyes from Ulrick's mocking, menacing gaze and looked at his cousin again. "The hell you sucking around here for? I paid you a hundred dollars for the tip about Fargo. To chew it fine, it wasn't even a tip. Fargo didn't come to poke her."

Hiram and Baylis erupted in derisive laughter.

"This is a 'poke her' establishment, ain't it?" Hiram taunted. "Well, mister, that's just what Fargo done. He poured the wood to Rosita until she was keening like a hired mourner."

"How in hell would you know that? Did he pay you to sketch them?"

"I jist followed old long shanks up the steps and stayed out on the landing with my ear to the door. Cuz, it was a sockdolager! That goddamn Fargo oughter charge him a stud fee."

Tutt waved this off although his face looked uncertain. "You and John Doe here are just angling for more money."

"Balls! I *heard* her, Cuz. She made a heap of doin's about the size of his tallywhacker"—Hiram was suddenly inspired to toss in another grizzly—"and made out how you was a needle dick. And when Fargo really got to pouring the cod to her? Why, Christ, she started babbling Mexer talk and screaming shit like '*Ay, mamacita!*' and '*Ay, caramba!*' She's a spitfire, all right."

Ulrick's lips curled back off his teeth as he watched Tutt mop the sweat off his forehead.

"That's malarkey," Tutt protested. "Hell, the sheriff went up there with them. His own deputy confirmed that."

"That's straight goods, but he didn't stay long. He almost caught me when he came out, and they wasn't doing the deed yet. That started almost right after he skedaddled."

Rage sparked in Tutt's eyes for a moment. Then they went dull and flat and calculating. He slid open a drawer and pulled out a bottle with the letters V.O.P. on the label. He poured the brandy into a pony glass and downed it in one gulp.

"Say, Frank," Baylis coaxed, "how's about pouring me and your cousin some of that popskull?"

"Popskull? This is Very Old Pale—bottled especially for army officers."

"Well, so what if it's for the high mucketys? Ain't polite to drink in front of others and not offer 'em a touch."

Tutt didn't give a tinker's damn right now about the liquor—not after hearing Hiram's description of Rosita in the throes of erotic pleasure. It didn't sound one bit made up. He slid the bottle across his desk to the other two.

"So exactly why are you two here?" he said impatiently. "I've got a business to run."

Hiram feigned amazement. "You mean to sit there and tell us that Fargo can prong your woman and you don't want the son of a bitch killed?"

Tutt's face tightened. "It's a man's natural instinct to go after quiff. It's the kept woman who violates the trust."

Hiram and Baylis hadn't expected this. They exchanged baffled glances. It was Baylis who spoke up. "We think Fargo ought to die."

"And I suppose I should pay you two to do it?"

"Why not?" Baylis asked. "You can sit there acting like he don't ruffle your feathers, but he's got you all consternated. We'll air out the bastard for a thousand dollars."

"A thou—? What the hell is wrong with you and what doctor told you so?"

"Easy, hoss," Baylis warned.

"Even if I wanted Fargo dead, why would I job it out to you when I have competent gunmen on my payroll? Besides, you know damn little about Skye Fargo if you think he's that easy to kill. He's hell on two sticks."

Baylis nodded. "We know that. That's why we have a special proposition for you. We all join forces. We go after him and your men go after him. If we kill him, you owe us the thousand. If you kill him, we get nothing. Nothing, that is, except the two thousand dollars you're going to have to pay us anyway."

Tutt gaped like a man who had woken up in the wrong country. "Fellow, has your brain gone soft? You two can't extort money from me."

"Actually," Baylis informed him emphatically, "there's four of us."

At first, Tutt's smooth, talcummed face registered only puzzlement. Then enlightenment came in a rush, and he looked as if he'd been drained by leeches.

"'At's right, bo," Baylis confirmed, "you're looking at one half of the Butcher Boys. Now you understand why it's important to get Fargo's life over, and pretty damn quick."

"You're fools to stick around here," Tutt said after swallowing hard. "After what you did to the Sloan family, if you're captured you won't even make it to trial."

Baylis sneered. "You think we don't know that, you perfumed asshole? We can't light out until Fargo is dead. Hiram tells me you got four men, all expert marksmen. With the four of us added. to the mix, that's eight men gunning for one. Even the Trailsman can't wangle out of those odds."

For a moment Tutt recalled Fargo's threat from last night, echoing in his memory with the force of Final Judgment: *If I find out you're feeding at the same trough as those murderers, you're going over the mountains.*

Tutt's lips trembled. "Boys, you don't rightly understand this thing. Right now I've got a sweet little deal going with the U.S. Army. Being linked to you would queer it."

"Funny you should mention that, Cuz," Hiram said, digging into his pocket and flashing a key with four bits instead of the usual one. "It's called a bar key. It'll open almost any door lock. Yesterday your beaner whore went out to a dress shop, and you was sleeping like a dead man. So I come for a little visit."

"That sweet little army deal you just mentioned," Baylis chimed in. "Did you check today to see if that little tin box is still under your bed?"

Tutt started, and now sweat flowed freely out of his pomaded hair.

Baylis laughed, enjoying this immensely. "'At's right, Frank, we got it. I know your kind. You figure there ain't room in the puddle but for one big frog, and *you're* that frog. The letters in that box will get you at least ten years in the territorial prison if we give them to the right jasper. Maybe a newspaper crusader, uh?"

"And don't forget, Cuz," Hiram said, "you only know two of us. That box is safely hid outside of town. You have your lick-fingers kill us, there'll be two left to put you in a world of shit. You won't catch the four of us together—when two are sleeping, the other two are on the prowl."

"See how it is?" Baylis said cheerfully. "We'll drop the fee for killing Fargo. Just cooperate with us in getting Fargo killed, slip us that two thousand, and we're out of your high-stacked hair forever. But if you refuse, or try to turn us around, you lose everything."

Tutt saw he was trapped. "All right. But at least keep your distance from me. If it ever gets out that I threw in with the Butcher Boys . . ."

The thought was so hideous that he couldn't finish it.

"That's jake by us," Baylis said. "Just remember: The quicker we snuff Fargo's wick, the better it is for all of us."

# 13

Fargo and Wade McKenna began their third day in the Santa Fe region by heading due west to check out Duro Canyon, the third robbers' roost the liveryman had told them about.

"Mr. Fargo," Wade said when they stopped to water their mounts at a spring, "you don't really expect them to be holed up in this canyon, do you?"

"Nah," Fargo said as he threw the Ovaro's bridle. "Sleeping rough ain't for board walkers like this bunch. These are men who starve and go naked without stores."

"How can you be sure?"

"I've had plenty of dealings with these unsavory types, soldier blue. A man who can stay alive on the frontier doesn't need to murder innocent ranchers. Besides, we already know they're trying to kill us—or me, anyway. That means keeping me in their sights, and they can't hardly do that from a canyon twenty miles west of town."

"Well, you've got me convinced. So why the hell are we bothering?"

"God save us all from West Point rangers," Fargo quipped. "When you sat on those benches, didn't your teachers talk about long-range strategy?"

"Of course," Wade bristled. "The battle is not the war."

"Same deal here. They say the mouse that has but one hole is quickly taken. Me and you're gonna make it hot for these bastards—mighty hot. And at some point they'll rabbit. These rides we've made to Los Hornos and Split Fork, this today— we're not wasting time, we're scouting and getting the lay of the land. I don't favor fighting in unscouted country. Nor should you, Lieutenant."

They pulled their horses back from the water. They grabbed

leather and pointed their bridles west at a long lope. Before them, the lush bottomland of the river valley rose gradually into folded hills dotted with stands of juniper and scrub pine.

The morning sun took on heat and weight as it rose behind them, throwing their long shadows out before them. All the New Mexico timber bothered Fargo, who vastly preferred the safety of open plains. It wasn't the Butcher Boys he worried about out here so much as Apaches. Although they holed up in northern Mexico, they liked to shoot north on quick raiding expeditions. And they were a tribe that favored the ambush.

Therefore, Fargo tried to keep his mind clear and rely only on his—and the Ovaro's—senses. Still, he could not crowd the thought of Corey Webster out of his mind completely. In conversation he said little about Corey now—no talk but in the doing. But that carved-up mess in the shack was an image that constantly cankered at him. This wasn't revenge he had embarked upon—it was hard, implacable justice and a duty owed to a man who had sacrificed so much to save a young man's life.

"The country's changing quick now," Wade called over to him.

Fargo nodded. The hills were more rugged now, dotted with wind-scrubbed knolls and granite spires, cut by runoff seams. Twenty minutes later they debouched from a thick stand of pine and spotted Duro Canyon.

"We'll ride around the lip," Fargo decided. "Stay to my left and keep a weather eye out. Best have your carbine to hand, too. If Apaches jump us, make every shot for score."

The canyon was neither as big nor as deep as Fargo would have expected in a roost. But soon enough, viewing it from the south wall, he realized why it was suited to outlaws. Although the canyon was mostly open and empty, the only entrance would force riders to single file through a narrow defile in the sandstone.

But that could prove suicidal if armed killers were waiting within—a tumble of large boulders on its west side provided excellent cover, and a huge limestone outcropping protected the boulders like a roof, discouraging fire from above.

"It's a natural breastwork," Fargo marveled. "I even see a seep spring down there."

Wade couldn't see as much as Fargo could. "See anybody down there?"

Fargo shook his head. "Can't get a good squint from here. Might be somebody waiting to douse our glims. But I think I can get closer. C'mon."

They rode to the lip of the west wall and Fargo lit down.

"Hobble that sorrel," he told Wade as he grabbed the hemp rope off his saddle horn. "Then come around to my stallion and hold his reins. When I give you the signal, walk him out slow. When I signal again, ease him back toward the canyon— but slow."

Wade's lips tightened with nervousness as he watched Fargo tie one end of the rope to the horn, the other around his waist.

"Isn't this risky, Mr. Fargo? I mean, what if something spooks your horse and he bolts? Or if he goes too far back, you could be left dangling right in those killer's sights."

Fargo grinned. "This pinto won't let anything happen to me—I pay for the oats."

The Ovaro's tail swished up fast and knocked Fargo's hat off.

He grinned. "Thanks, old campaigner. I needed to leave that behind anyway."

He looked at Wade. "Don't worry. He's smart as a steel trap and he likes you. Just guide him out by the bridle. When you walk him back, just face the canyon and talk low in his ear. If it's empty down there, I'll just sing out when I want to be pulled up. If I see something, I'll tug the rope."

"All right," Wade said uncertainly. "But that's a lot of faith to put in a horse."

"This from a man who swore an oath to a government."

Fargo moved up to the lip of the outcropping and waved to McKenna before sprawling out flat on his stomach. He waved again when the rope tightened. As the Ovaro moved backward at the perfect pace, Fargo knocked the riding thong off the hammer of his Colt and shucked it out.

He slid down the edge of the shelf until he had a good view of the space under it. As he'd expected, just the usual detritus of a robber's roost: rusted airtights, charred wood, an old boot and other castoff clothing. He gave the hail to Wade and was soon on his feet again topside.

"Nothing," he reported to Wade. "But there's a chance they could be using it and just aren't here. Let's go read some sign."

They found the rocky slope that led down to the narrow defile. Fargo, dangling low in the saddle, studied the dirt at the entrance to the cave. "No sign of men, red or white," he said. "Only coyote and bear tracks, and they're old. Nobody's used this place for a long time."

He looked at Wade. "Like I said, we'll find our Butcher Boys in the City of Holy Faith."

Fargo rested the palm of his hand on his Colt. "And right here's our warrant."

The two men returned to Santa Fe by late afternoon. They left their horses at the livery and locked their rifles in Manuel's gun cabinet. Then they walked back toward the center of town, eyes gliding to all sides.

"The best way to cure a boil is to lance it," Fargo told the officer. "We'll get nothing done by holing up in our room. The more we show ourselves around town, the better our chances they'll try to sink us."

"You mean we're the bait in the trap?"

Fargo's strong white teeth flashed through his beard. "More like the meat that feeds the tiger. You sure you don't want to go back to safe desk duty, kid?"

"Are you joshing? Play stoopenfetchit for Harding? I'll get plenty of that soon enough, but I won't likely ever get another chance to side the Trailsman."

"Just don't pick the bullet side. All right, let's start by stoking our bellies. Them damn slices of egg-dipped toast we had at the hotel for breakfast were tasty enough, but you could grow slat-ribbed on that kind of old-lady grub."

They ducked into a little café on Calle Mayor and ordered steaks with all the trimmings. Fargo kept his back to a wall while he ate, eyes at attention each time the door opened.

Wade sopped up the last of his gravy with a blue corn tortilla. "Should I get another hat? I like this one, but you're right—it's not Western garb."

"Good idea. Give us an opportunity to take in some air," Fargo remarked with double meaning. He added, "Of course, we don't want to 'take in' *too* much air—or sunlight."

Wade hung fire for a few moments, fishing for the meaning of this pun. When he finally caught it he turned slightly pale, and Fargo laughed. "Just a little gallows humor, junior. You won't survive out here without it."

The boardwalk was thronged when they left the café, and Fargo narrowed his eyes in the bright, late-afternoon glare, keeping his eyes on hands as much as faces. Wade replaced his felt derby with a low-crowned hat featuring a wide brim like Fargo's.

"Could be we're in the wrong part of town for trapping rats," Fargo said as they left the haberdasher's. "Let's cut over to Silver Street and cut the dust."

"Is that the rough part of town?"

"Sure wager you won't find Leora Padgett sipping cider there. Locals claim they have a man for breakfast every day on Silver Street. I saw a man gunned down for farting in a saloon. Don't try to take down that who-shot-john they serve unless you put water behind it—it could drop a buffalo bull in his tracks. Better yet, we'll order beer if they have it. And for Christ sakes, none of your pissing fights. Remember, we're trying to draw out trouble, not make it."

Fargo turned down a rutted street that stank of rotten meat and human sewage. Unlike most of Santa Fe, which was built with adobe and tiles, the saloons, crude eating houses, and "hog ranches" as locals called cathouses on Silver Street, were mostly dilapidated, unpainted plank structures. There were even a few tents.

"Don't be gawking," Fargo warned McKenna. "These filthy, snake-eyed jaspers watching us are pure vermin, and if you fall asleep at the switch they'll kill you for your new hat. Besides, any of them could be the exact same vermin we're looking to exterminate."

Fargo slapped open the rickety batwings of a tumble-down saloon called the Black Cat. The two men paused for a moment so their eyes could adjust to the dim, smoky interior. The stench made Fargo curl his toes.

"Two beers," he told the bar dog, "and draw one nappy."

Fargo used the cracked and blurry back-bar mirror to check out the patrons. The place was about half full, many of the men taking his measure from lidded gazes. He noticed several tie-down guns.

"Rouse out your gelt, gents," the bartender said. "Two beers will be four bits."

Beer was widely sold at only a dime a glass and Wade opened his mouth to complain. But Fargo spiked him in the ribs with his elbow as he planked a handful of half-dime pieces. He headed toward an empty table along the left wall, scowling at Wade.

"You goddamn fool," he said quietly. "Ain't you learned by now there's no education in the second kick of a mule? You got your clock cleaned on the boardwalk when we first got to town, and you're *still* on the scrap?"

"Ahh . . . but that bartender is a thief! Beer is—"

"Put a sock in it. You don't like the price, walk out. Like I already told you, only pick fights that matter. Bar dogs in watering holes like this usually keep an express gun under the counter. I may not be a landowner, soldier blue, but I place a higher value on my life than fifteen cents."

Chairs got busted up quick in holes like this one and the two men had to settle for empty nail kegs. Fargo was still settling in when the batwings exploded inward and a mustachioed, hard-eyed character with a low-slung gun belt stepped inside. He surveyed the smoky interior, his eyes lingering on everyone except Fargo.

"He came in almost right behind us," Wade said, wiping foam off his upper lip with his sleeve. "Like maybe he was following us. Think he's one of the Butcher Boys?"

Fargo studied him for a few moments and then shook his head. "Nah. I been shooing his type off my heels for a long time. He's a jobber, a hired killer, and that breed are loners. But even though he's not a Butcher Boy, I'd say he's got murder on his mind. We'll find out short meter."

"Murder? Us?"

"Most likely just me. Killing a soldier is harder to get away with."

"Hunh," Wade said. "So the gang decided to hire it out. Wonder where they got the money."

"I think our four killers will do their own work," Fargo opined. "A hired killer might do their dirt work and then turn them in for the reward. They don't call these professional gunmen mercenaries for nothing."

Fargo watched the swaggering, confident, stone-eyed man pay for a bottle and leave the glass on the counter. He glanced around the saloon, evidently picking a good spot to sit down.

Wade's smooth-shaven face was a mask of confusion. "I don't understand. If the Butcher Boys—" Sudden enlightenment dawned in his eyes. "Oh, yeah. Tutt."

"That's just a guess, mind you. I haven't been in town long enough to piss off anybody else—'cept maybe that weasel-dick hotel clerk, and I doubt he's got enough rocks in his pocket to hire a chimney sweep."

Fargo glanced around, gauging the faces of the men watching the new arrival.

"If this is Tutt's hireling," Fargo added, "I'd wager he's not one of Tutt's reg'lar gun toughs. The men here are eyeing him up like he's a stranger—same way they did us. He was hired just to kill me and ride on. Makes me feel what you call *significant*."

"There's your gallows humor again."

The stranger in question made a big show of swaggering to the empty table nearest Fargo although still studiously ignoring him.

"Jesus," Wade said quietly, studying the mother-of-pearl butt of the man's Remington .50. "Is Tutt *that* jealous?"

Fargo recalled his conversations with the tempting Rosita. "Jealous, no. He doesn't care a jackstraw about Rosita. But greedy men like him don't share, and I tapped *his* private stock."

All that was true, and Fargo knew of men who killed for far less. Still, even though he couldn't make sense of it yet, he suspected this killer might have been hired for a different reason—one that eluded him at present.

Three poor Mexican braceros, evidently without jobs, judging from their frayed, raw wool serapes and rope sandals, sat at the table between Fargo and the hired gun.

"Hey, Sancho!" the new arrival called loudly to the one facing him, getting the attention of everyone in the saloon.

*"Sí, jefe?"*

"When you Mexicans fuck your mothers, do you call them by your sister's name or your horse's?"

The men, none of whom appeared to be armed, read the clear warning in the man's mean, hateful face. Without a word they finished their cactus liquor and got up and left.

"And stay out, chilipeps!" he taunted behind them. "I will not abide a beaner."

Fargo, calmly sipping his beer and waiting for the fandango, saw that Wade was silently fuming. "Steady in the ranks, Lieutenant," he said casually, and the shavetail settled down.

Fargo belched loudly. He knew this would provoke the hired gun, and almost immediately he spoke up.

"You, with the beard. Wild savages wear buckskins. What tribe you and your papoose with, Chief?"

Fargo had been goaded by enough tinhorn killers over the years to know this was the start of the usual insults intended to make him draw down. That way it could look like a "fair fight" if the law poked into it. However, he shared one thing in common with the men of West Point: He never let his enemies set the rules of engagement.

"Just curious, stout lad," he replied cheerfully. "How much did Tutt pay you to kill me?"

The saloon abruptly went as silent and still as a graveyard at midnight. The bully flinched, clearly startled. But he quickly recovered his sneer of cold command. "Nobody mentioned killing."

"I just did. How much, Tumbledown Dick? A man likes to know what he's worth on the open market."

"You might want to rein in that tongue of yours, Dan'l Boone. I ain't one for arm wrasslin'."

"You a pull-down killer or a back-shooter?" Fargo pressed. "Or both."

"Right now, buckskin boy, you're standing on your own grave."

The bullyboy pushed to his feet and Fargo, still seated, laughed. "Shit! Ain't you a holy show? I've scraped better men than you off my boots. An Apache wouldn't waste a bullet on you—he'd kill you with a rock."

By now everyone around them had moved to clear a ballistics path. "The winner leaves five bucks for the undertaker," the bartender called out in a business-as-usual tone.

"Get up, mouthpiece!" the hired gun ordered Fargo.

Fargo, smiling with pleasure at this little game, shook his head. "I don't stand up to kill a roach. Go ahead, chumley, slap it."

"I said stand up, you cockchafer!" The thug was clearly unnerved by Fargo's breezy manner. His breathing had grown hoarse and raggedy.

Fargo's teeth flashed through his beard when he laughed. "S'matter, Gertrude? Getting all excited and emotional like this. Maybe you should take up sewing to calm your nerves. Or maybe you need a boyfriend?"

The gunman's Remington was only halfway out of the holster when Fargo's Colt seemed to leap into his fist. Its single, unblinking eye stared into the whey-faced man's frightened visage.

He swallowed audibly. "Jesus, mister! Did that goddamn thing pop out of your sleeve?"

"Run along and play now," Fargo told him. "And I advise you to hop your horse and light a shuck out of Santa Fe. If I see you again I'll kill you for cause."

The man nodded once and beat a hasty retreat.

"Holy Hanna!" Wade said, still trying to get his own breathing under control. "I didn't know you were that fast, Mr. Fargo. You had me on the ragged edge."

"I'm not all that fast. That's why I always rattle a man's confidence first if I can."

"Why didn't you kill him? He drew first and he sure's hell meant to kill you."

"This ain't a shilling shocker," Fargo replied. "For one thing, you were too stupid to move out of the way. And powder-burning a man in a public place can get complicated, starting with that five-dollar undertaker's fee. I only bury my friends."

Wade looked skeptical. "Are those the real reasons?"

"Of course not. I was eager to irrigate his guts—kill one fly, kill a million. But finding Corey's killers comes first, and if I'd a blown this son of a bitch through the wall it would

**106**

have to get back to Sheriff Kinkaid. This would be my second killing in town, and he's just itching to jug me."

Wade nodded. "Yeah, I take your drift. Man, I *should* have a notebook. This was exciting."

Fargo pushed to his feet and grabbed his hat. "Yeah? Pretty damn quick now, soldier blue, you're gonna have a lot more excitement than you bargained for."

# 14

Rosita knew that a trouble storm was brewing. Bad trouble for her.

She first realized it when Tutt did not go downstairs, as usual, to gamble and mingle with his important customers. Instead, he slept until only ten o'clock and then dressed and settled in the parlor with a bottle of the Very Old Pale he received shipments of from Major Harding. By two p.m., when she began dressing for her usual shopping excursion, he was dangerously drunk.

"Where the hell do you think you're going?" he demanded when she came into the parlor for her black lace shawl. Even on the hottest days, women in Santa Fe never appeared in public without an outer garment.

"To College Street," she replied, alarmed by his puffy face and heavy-lidded eyes. Some men could not hold their liquor, and Frank was one of them.

"You're a four-flushing liar," he said in a low, ominous voice. "You're going to Fargo's hotel room so that mangy drifter can rut on you like he did the other night."

"*Vaya, loco!* He came here only to ask some questions about the Sloan killings."

Tutt's sneer twisted into a mask of violent hatred. She felt his next words with the force of slaps. "You vile twat, I had a man outside the door. He heard all of it."

Fear made her pulse quicken until she could feel it throbbing in her palms. "Then he is a liar as are most of your hirelings!"

"Yeah, you flare them nostrils at me, you tawny bitch. Don't come the haughty ingénue with me, I know *all* your parlor tricks. Including the ones you showed Fargo. That little cunny of yours can bark, yodel, and juggle, hey? I hear you especially liked Fargo's size? Biggest damn cod you ever saw, huh?"

She felt desperation welling inside her. Rosita had seen him like this only once before, when he suspected her of dallying with a handsome soldier. That time, she had come within a hairsbreadth of dying. She should have fled then. This time it might be too late.

"Frank, you have had too much to drink—it makes you mean."

Tutt snorted. "No, no, Mexican girl, you got it bass ackwards. I'm just 'inebriate of the senses' as the poets say. You know . . . drunk on life and all that shit."

"Frank, these foolish men of yours have filled your mind with *basura*, trash. And I do not even know what this word ingénue means. Or this word in—ineber—*que palabra tan difícil!*"

"Yeah, change the subject, you cunning little whore. I notice how your command of English always deteriorates when you're lying your tight little ass off. That's a trick all you chilipeps use."

"Well, I know that only a man would make up such a lie about size—women do not notice such things."

He sat forward in a velvet-upholstered wing chair and poured himself another glass. "In a pig's ass, you lying bitch. You've told *me* I have an impressive size on me."

"All women say this to all men. We do not care, but we know you men worry about such little things."

Too late she realized her poor choice of words. Tutt snarled like a rabid animal, threw his drink to the floor, and flew out of the chair. He lunged for her, hands just missing her neck when she neatly sidestepped him.

"Little things? So you're throwing it in my goddamn face?" he bellowed like a burned bear. "Telling me I'm short-dicking you but Fargo's equipped like a studhorse? Right here under my roof where you live for free and have two closets stuffed with the best gowns available anywhere on the King's Highway?"

She edged toward the door leading to the landing and the backstairs. "*Eres borracho*, you are drunk, very drunk."

"Yeah, goddamn but you're astute. And you're also a

back-alley whore who sneaks greasy drifters upstairs and lets 'em pound you like a spike maul."

Rosita was so scared by now that a corroded-pennies taste crept into her throat. Tutt was a deadly bomb with a very short fuse, and her only chance was to make it to that door before he could.

"Frank, *lo juro*, I swear it. Fargo did not touch me. He—"

She suddenly lunged for the door, but Tutt was surprising agile for a man so "inebriate of the senses."

"No, you don't, you treacherous slut!" He slammed her against the door, her arms pinioned. "Don't play the larks with me, *chiqitina*. Fargo slipped under your chemise, and you think *I'm* taking his leavings?"

"Frank, let me—"

"Shut your cakehole. No decent goddamn woman would give that worthless son of a bitch the time of day. But you brought him up to *my* place and played bucking bronco on his rodeo pole, huh? Diddled him in *my* goddamn bed and probably didn't even have the goddamn common courtesy to change the linen!"

He slapped her so hard her teeth clacked together. Rosita had been frightened up to this point, but her fiery Latin blood suffused her cheeks in a burst of indignant rage.

"It was not the bed, Frank. We could not wait that long after Fargo watched me strip naked for Sheriff Kinkaid. We did it in the very chair where you were just sitting. But unlike you, Fargo did not simply grunt after the first one and go to sleep. He kept going and going—I am still sore from that magnificent man!"

These words struck Tutt like canister shot, and he staggered back, letting go of Rosita. This was her perfect chance to escape and she flung the door open—only to encounter Brad Matlock grinning at her, his Colt to hand.

"Best go back in, Rosy," he advised her in his hillman's twang. "You got mighty fine catheads on you, but old Frank pays me in gold cartwheels. I don't *even* want to kill you."

Reluctantly she shut the door, deeply regretting her outburst to Frank. He still looked like a man who had taken too much opium.

"Kinkaid?" he repeated. "You stripped buck for Kinkaid while Fargo watched? *Two* of them? That means you let both of them bull you!"

Rosita edged around him and laid hands on a solid brass lamp. "Do not be foolish, Frank. I said those crazy things because I was angry."

"No, you sick and disgusting whore of Babylon. You only tell the truth when you're pissed off."

He lunged at her again and she threw the lamp at his head. Her aim was bad and he managed to knock it aside with both hands, grunting at the pain. Rosita saw the homicidal glint in his mad eyes and backed across the room, grabbing anything she could and hurling it at him.

"Both of them," he repeated in an incredulous voice even as he ducked a heavy ashtray. "Gelding me under my own roof. Better start with them Hail Marys, bitch, because Jesus will soon be here to cover you with a blanket."

An hour of sunlight still remained as Fargo and McKenna searched out their next seedy watering hole on Silver Street. When Fargo, tensed for trouble, heard his name called out from behind, he crouched and whirled around, Colt cocked and ready.

Deputy Pedro Valdez froze in midstep, hands going out to his sides. "*Por Dios!* Do not shoot me, Senor Fargo. I have not changed my underdrawers today, and this will shame my mother."

Fargo looked at the kid and they both laughed at the same time.

"Sorry, Pedro," Fargo said as he leathered his shooter. "But this isn't the best place to approach a man from behind."

"I would not trouble you, but . . . *pues*, it is Rosita."

"What about her?"

Pedro took off his straw hat and rotated it in his fingers. "I think Tutt is about to kill her."

"No offense, but if that's the straight shouldn't *you* be doing something about it? You're the deputy, duly sworn."

Pedro shook his head. "Nothing is what it seems in Santa Fe, Senor Fargo. The city charter, it calls for an Anglo sheriff and a Mexican deputy. What this truly means is that Sheriff Kinkaid is the law for whites and I am the law for Mexicans."

"Last time I saw her," Fargo said, "Rosita was a Mexican. Has somebody bleached her?"

Pedro laughed and nodded. "A good one, Senor Fargo. *Claro* she is a Mexican, but Frank Tutt is not. He is one of *los ricos*, the wealthy, in Santa Fe, and Rosita is his property."

Fargo scratched his beard, not liking this at all. "In other words, if you interfere Tutt's pistoleros will give you a case of lead poisoning."

Pedro nodded. "The sheriff, he is serving a warrant down in Madrid."

Fargo definitely didn't like this. He wasn't some kind of damn knight in shining armor. He had already figured out that he and Tutt would be locking horns soon enough, but not over this. Fargo's mind kept things in separate cabinets—he had already put the horns on Tutt, and Fargo wasn't eager to compound the crime. On the other hand . . .

"How do you know he's killing her?" Fargo asked as all three men began hurrying toward the center of town.

"I have a—how do you say?—case on her," Pedro confessed. "I heard a rumor today about Tutt, how he was so angry with her that he did not come downstairs to gamble. When Tutt does not gamble it is time to expect trouble. So I went to the alley behind his gambling house and—*que rudioso tan grande!*—what a racket! They are destroying the place."

"Any idea what caused this ruckus?"

Pedro cast his eyes downward—an eloquent enough reply.

Fargo heaved a reluctant sigh. Rosita was one more fine page in his big book of love, but it was turning into a mare's nest. Still—a man shouldn't step in anything he can't wipe off.

"Where's his gun throwers?" Fargo asked, stepping up the pace as they turned onto the main street.

"Two are inside the saloon as always. Only one guards the rear door."

Fargo figured there was only one because Tutt had him figured for a corpse right about now.

"This man," Valdez continued, "is Brad Matlock. He hates Mexicans and would shoot me if I tried to go up the stairs. He is a killer but not so—how you say?—unreasonable as the others.

He does not like Tutt, and Rosita has been . . . kind to him and he likes her. I think he would welcome you going up there. And, of course, he is not stupid and he knows who you are."

"Wade," Fargo said as they neared the Gilded Cage, "run on ahead and cut into the alley. Then come down from the south end and make sure Matlock sees you. Christ sakes, don't threaten him or draw your weapon. Just keep him distracted long enough for me to get the drop on him. Pedro, you better fade now."

Fargo cut into the alley in the grainy twilight and waited behind a stack of shipping crates until Wade had drawn near. At least Rosita was still alive—he could hear loud curses and the breaking of glass even from the alley. When Fargo heard the guard challenge Wade, he filled his hand and darted toward the steps.

"Brad!" he called out. "It's Fargo and I've got you notched! How's about a gentleman's agreement so I can help Rosita?"'

"Skye Goldang Fargo! Say, this is a pure-dee pleasure. You know, I go to this astrological doctor a couple blocks over. She told me that today is a very important day for making careful decisions. Well . . . here's our story. I *tried* to shoot your ass, but this cracked firing pin in my short iron bollixed me up."

As Matlock said all this he was thudding fast down the stairs, gun holstered. "Best hurry, Fargo," he added. "Tutt is all wound up to a fare-thee-well. Rosita has been holding him off, but he's doing that crazy breathing and deep shouting like men do before they go into a kill frenzy."

Brad scuttled off, and Fargo told the kid to guard the stairs. He gained the landing and pushed the door open, gun in hand. His eyes widened in astonishment—one lamp had not been broken and its glow revealed a path of destruction to equal a cyclone. Broken glass and pottery lay in shards everywhere, furniture was buckled, books and papers and clothing were scattered broadcast.

A man's screech of agony pulled Fargo into the back bedroom. Tutt, a sharp letter opener in his right fist, straddled Rosita on the floor. But he was in no condition to skewer her because she had his balls in a ferocious squeeze.

"End of trail," Fargo announced and Rosita loosened her

**113**

grip. Tutt sent Fargo a startled, over-the-shoulder glance, and Fargo confirmed what he had already guessed.

"'S'matter, Tutt? Seen a ghost?"

Tutt, breathing heavy like a man in rut, managed only, "Don't know . . . what . . . you mean."

"Save it for your memoirs. By the way—I don't think you'll be seeing your imported gun. I convinced him the air was better elsewhere. Next time, spend more than thirty-five cents."

"If you're . . . implying I hired . . . someone to kill—"

"Bottle it. I'll settle accounts with you later. What the hell are you doing thumping all over Rosita? I told you I only came up here for information. Rosita didn't—"

"I told him, Skye," Rosita cut in. "Get off me, you disgusting lump of shit!" she fumed, rolling Tutt off of her. "He knows everything. About how I stripped for the sheriff, about how we did it in the chair—how I praised your size."

There was great satisfaction in her voice. Fargo, on the other hand, felt like a fool. "Well, hell," he said, disgust in his voice, "let's just send for a newspaper scribbler."

He looked at Tutt. "All right, so what, asshole? I screwed Rosita and you tried to kill me. I don't call that an honest cipher—she's not your wife. Rosita?"

He helped her to her feet and watched her try to straighten her dress. "Yes?"

"Since rooster crest here knows, you realize you'll have to leave Santa Fe, right?"

"Of course. The pig will have me killed."

"Whore," Tutt snarled, unable to stand yet.

"This from a *cabrón* with acorns for nuts!"

"Don't start that shit," Fargo cut in. "Just lower your hammers. Rosita, do you have a place to go?"

"Yes, my—"

"Keep it dark," Fargo warned. "Is there money up here?"

"Yes."

"All right, throw some clothes into a valise and take a hotel room tonight. There's an Overland office in town. You can leave tomorrow. If this leading citizen sends anyone to harm you, I'll smoke him down. I owe him that much anyway, and as soon as I fill in some pieces, me and him are going to be huggin'."

"Fargo, you can't prove—"

"Prove a cat's tail. C'mon, Rosita, get a wiggle on."

When she was ready, Fargo said, "All right, take the front stairs down through the club. I'll stay up here with red crest and make sure he doesn't follow you."

"Thank you, Skye," Rosita said, "you may wear rough clothing, but you are a gentleman *de veras*."

She turned her fierce dark eyes on Tutt. "As for *this* gringo piece of—"

"Fight's over," Fargo reminded her. "Have a nice trip to Mexico."

After the door slammed behind her, Tutt managed to drag himself onto the bed, still clutching his groin. "You did me a favor, Fargo. I'm rid of the bitch now."

"I did her the favor," Fargo remarked absently, his mind on something else. "That killer you sicced on me today— was jealousy your only motive?"

"I don't hire killers."

"All right, and I can make cheese out of chalk. If it turns out that jealousy made you do it, I'll let it go. You're a prideful man, and after all I did wrong coming up here and all. But if there's more to it, Tutt, I guarandamntee you'll be in one world of shit before I leave Santa Fe."

"You're just shooting at rovers," Tutt said, averting his eyes from Fargo's penetrating blue gaze.

Fargo went back out to the door on the landing and eased it open a few inches. Wade dutifully stood watch below, an indistinct form in the gathering darkness.

"What's the weather out there like?" he called down.

"Looks clear, but this whole alley is lined with crates and barrels."

Fargo stepped out and pulled the door shut behind him. The rise-and-fall drone of insects filled the alley, which seemed deserted from up here. He shucked out his Colt and thumbed it to full cock, starting down the steps.

"Is Rosita still alive?" Wade called up to him.

"Sassy as ever. But Tutt may never sire another bastard."

Fargo was halfway down when he noticed something felt wrong.

But what?

The gravelly voice that sounded a memory chord belonged to his first wilderness mentor, Corey Webster, speaking words that had saved Fargo's life more than once: *When the insect noise stops suddenlike, tadpole, trouble is only a fox step away.*

As it had stopped just now. Fargo went into a deep crouch on the steps only a fractional second before a hammering racket of gunfire exploded the peace of the alley.

Bullets sent plumes of adobe dust spouting from the wall where, a moment before, Fargo had stood in plain view.

"God-in-whirlwinds!" Wade exclaimed, but the shavetail didn't panic. He began sending rounds toward a freight wagon parked on the opposite side of the alley. Fargo followed his aim and sent more lead to the party. Briefly, he glimpsed two shadowy figures bolting between a warehouse and a black-smith shop. They tossed snap shots over their shoulders to cover their retreat.

"Ease off, kid!" Fargo barked when Wade started to give chase.

"But this is our chance, Mr. Fargo! They're close enough to spit on."

Fargo reached the ground and started thumbing reloads into his Colt. "You didn't even fill your wheel, you dumb shit. And anyhow, you shouldn't take bait like that. Don't they teach about the pincer's trap at West Point? It's a favorite of these raffish types."

"You mean—these two could just be a lure?"

"Why not? And if it's the Butcher Boys that leaves two more waiting to air us out. Never give your enemy the whip hand."

The two men played it safe and cut over to the crowded main street as they headed for their hotel.

"You sure it was the Butcher Boys?" Wade asked. "That killer in the Black Cat sure wasn't one of them."

"No, I'm not sure. I tend to draw trouble and it gets damn hard to winnow the grain from the chaff. We need information."

Fargo glanced into the darkling sky, already star shot. "Moon's in full phase tonight. I think the two of us need to hit the grub pile and then take a little ride."

# 15

The two men stoked up on eggs and chorizo, spiced sausage, at a café near the Dorsey House. Fargo hoped to spot Leora Padgett's blond coif in the lobby, but she was nowhere to be seen. However, Sheriff Hank Kinkaid was sprawled in a leather chair, his face dour and ominous. The deepening network of creases around his eyes and mouth seemed etched even deeper.

"So what is it, Fargo?" he greeted the Trailsman. "Are you trying to overturn an election and take over my job?"

"The hell? If you're talking about that deal with Rosita and Tutt, you were out of town. Would you prefer that I let her be killed? And that little ambush in the alley was none of my doing."

"Hell, that ain't what I mean. And you done a good job with that two-bit hire-a-holster in the Black Cat. Matter fact, you had every right to kill him based on what I heard."

Fargo shrugged. "Then what's your dicker?"

"Son, don't stand there and piss in my boots. You know damn well what my dicker is. This Butcher Boys deal is an open case. That means only law enforcement has a right to poke into it."

"Sure, but have you poked?"

Kinkaid's weathered face took on a purple tinge. "That's none a your damn business."

"How are me and Wade getting in your way?"

"Well, for starters, how 'bout them damn owlhoots you sent to Silver Street last night? I hear them sons a bitches was acting like Pinkerton men."

Fargo shot a quick look at Wade. The sheriff had to mean Ace Ludlow and his bunch.

"You do know," Kinkaid added, his eyes narrowing, "that consorting with known outlaws is a crime?"

"Consorting is a word that needs to be chewed finer," Fargo said.

"Let me chew it finer then. I don't know who this bunch is, and nobody on Silver Street will tell me. But if you know their names, and they're wanted for crimes, you got no choice but to turn that information over to me."

"I don't mean to spout like a Philadelphia lawyer," Fargo said, "but you're right only if I *know* they're wanted. I've seen no wanted dodgers nor newspaper stories about them."

Kinkaid looked at Wade. "Boy, you took a viper to your breast when you threw in with this hombre. He can sidestep almost anything, but an army officer is on the straight and narrow. You'd be wise to cut your tether from him before you end up in the stockade."

"I appreciate the warning, Sheriff," Wade said courteously, leaving it there.

Kinkaid looked at Fargo again. "You got to understand this thing, Fargo. This butchering of the Sloan women has this territory in an uproar. The governor is trying like hell to establish law and order, to put the quietus on all this vigilante shit. If you just sashay on in and free these killers from their souls, without so much as a trial or even a by-your-leave, it will encourage others to take the law into their own hands."

"I'm no crusader," Fargo objected. "It's the newspapers you need to go after, not me. I work within the law."

"Like hell you do. If that was true, you'd stop canvassing the country and enlisting outlaws to your cause. In fact, you'd just *stop*, period. Matter fact, that's what I'm ordering you to do right now, both of you. Just keep your damn noses out of the pie and let the law handle this."

Fargo suddenly looked innocent as a cherub. "I'm not one to buck an honest lawman, Kinkaid, and I'm told you're middling honest. But sometimes I don't hear so good."

Kinkaid looked at Wade. "How 'bout you, kid? Can *you* hear?"

*"No hable ingles,"* McKenna replied, and Fargo had to

bite his lower lip to keep a straight face. He liked this tender-foot a little more each day.

Kinkaid expelled a fluming sigh. "Well, I done my level best. But for Christ sakes, Fargo, if you're bound and determined to mix into this thing, try not to parade it. The governor is worried sick that vigilantes are going to take over here like they already done out in the Sierra."

These last words caught Fargo flat-footed. It sounded like the tough old lawman was changing his tune somewhat. Kinkaid pushed to his feet, grunting at the effort.

"I take your drift, Sheriff," was all Fargo said.

"I don't get it," Wade said, watching the burly man's retreating back. "He orders us to steer wide of the Butcher Boys, then tells us to be discreet about it."

Fargo tugged at his beard, pondering it. "What we have here, I suspect, is an honest man trying to do his duty. He mentioned the governor, who's right here in Santa Fe. I think Kinkaid was called in and had his ass reamed—and he doesn't like the way he was treated. So he passed on the warning to us, with a wink and a nod."

The two men spent the next hour in their room playing joker poker for low stakes.

"I think it's late enough," Fargo finally announced.

"For that little ride you mentioned?"

Fargo nodded, strapping his shell belt back on. "We need to check in the fork of that lightning-split tree north of town. Ace Ludlow said he'd leave a note there if him or his gang found out anything."

Wade gathered up the cards, his face skeptical. "You, of all people, trust a criminal to smoke out other criminals?"

"You heard the sheriff—outlaws were asking questions about the Butcher Boys. And Ace and his boys don't exactly hitch at the same tie-rail with killers like the Butcher Boys. C'mon, let's get horsed and head out there."

Santa Fe nightlife was just getting into full stride as the two men walked south toward Manuel's livery. The board-walk was crowded and Fargo watched hands not faces, his own right hand poised near his holster. They now had two factions to worry about, the Butcher Boys and Tutt's paid killers. Fargo wasn't sure Tutt had the sand to continue his shoot-to-kill order once his blood cooled off—then again, Fargo had packed his favorite night woman off to Mexico, fuel on fuel to the fires raging within Tutt.

Fargo sighed. "It's live and let live, with me," he told Wade. "How can such a lovable cuss always have his dingus in the wringer?"

Wade gave an exaggerated shrug. "Why ask me? I'm fresh off ma's milk."

At the southern outskirts of town, beyond the range of the streetlamps, shadows dominated. But a full moon and a star-shot sky assisted Fargo's danger-trained eyes as he inspected the paddock and the area around the barn.

"Looks clear," he told Wade. "Besides, none of the dogs are raising a ruckus."

They did, however, as the two men approached and Manuel appeared almost immediately with a scattergun held muzzle down under his right arm.

"Don't fire that widow maker, Manuel," the Trailsman called out. "We just have to make a little night ride."

*"Claro, Senor Fargo,"* the liveryman replied. "With such a fine Ovaro in my paddock, I must be cautious. Many men have asked me to sell him to them."

Fargo mulled that. By now there were a pack of two-legged curs in Santa Fe who might realize that killing the Ovaro would place his owner at a serious disadvantage.

"Tell you what, old-timer. When I bring him back tonight, I'm gonna stall him even though he hates it. And you best keep him stalled nights from now on."

The two men lugged their saddles and bridles from the tack room and rigged their horses while Manuel unlocked their rifles. In the light of a coal-oil lantern they inspected each foot—hoof, pastern, and fetlock—carefully. Then they forked leather and headed north.

Fargo figured they had waited late enough to discourage any dry gulchers along the trail. He also kept a wary eye on their back trail to make sure they weren't being followed. The Ovaro kept fighting the bit, wanting to stretch out the kinks, so Fargo opened him out from a trot to a canter to a gallop and finally a full run, the Ovaro's muscles working like well-oiled machinery.

"Jesus," Wade said when his cavalry sorrel finally caught up after Fargo slowed the stallion, "you should call that horse the Coal Torpedo!"

"Ah, he's a mite better than a farm nag," Fargo allowed, and the Ovaro nickered in protest.

Soon the shadowy mass of the big cottonwood appeared to the right of the trail. Fargo reined in and flipped the reins forward over the Ovaro's head to hold him in place. He swung down and approached the tree cautiously, blue steel filling his right hand. When he judged it was safe, he plunged his left hand into the jagged split, encountering paper.

"There's something in here, all right," he called back to Wade.

It was folded a few times. Fargo took it back out onto the trail where the moonlight was better. Leathering his Colt he pulled a lucifer from his possibles bag and thumb-scratched it to life, unfolding the foolscap sheet. It was an advertisement for men's hernia trusses. Fargo flipped it over and found a hastily scrawled note:

> *The bucherr what dun fir yer pard is namd Bayliss Ulrik. Sumbudy in his gang liks to swill whisskey and shoot off his mouth. Wun of the shitstains siding him is a peece of locul trash namd Hirum Steel, a ratty litel bassturd with a fas lik a cratur. Staing in town, but we dont no wher.*

Fargo had to burn a second match to struggle through the poorly spelled missive.

The p.s. leaped out at him and quickened his pulse: *Steel is Frank Tutt's cuzin.*

Fargo read it aloud for the kid. "So *that's* the gait," he mused when he finished. "This doesn't exactly prove it, but there's a damn good chance that Tutt and the Butcher Boys are feeding at the same trough."

"That or it's one hell of a coincidence," Wade said. "What I don't get, though, is why a rich man like Tutt with a going business and all would throw in with men who butcher women."

Fargo nodded as he poked the note into his pocket. "That's a stumper, all right. Any man linked to those hyenas is marked for carrion bait. I'm the last man to defend Tutt, but I never really believed he'd put a killer on me just because I topped his woman."

Fargo grabbed the horn and swung up onto the hurricane deck. Instead of reining around, however, he sat there in the moonlight digesting this new information.

"Baylis Ulrick, huh?" he finally said in a purposeful tone, as if searing the name onto a tombstone. "All right, then. Hell ain't *half* full, Mr. Baylis goddamn Ulrick."

Fargo hated like hell to put a horse away wet, so they held a slow trot back to town, each man's eyes scouring the sides of the trail. They rubbed their mounts down with old feed sacks, led them to the water trough, then stalled them, forking hay into the stalls before they left.

"Damn," Wade remarked of the busy street, "don't they ever go to bed around here?"

"Oh, they go to bed," Fargo quipped, "but they don't go home very early. This is the world-beatingest town. First Indian, then Spanish, then Mexican, now American—hell, I figure the Russians will claim it next. The people don't give a damn. They just change the flag and go on being Santa Fe."

A weaving drunk aimed at them, and both men drew their guns.

"Jehoshaphat!" He sobered in a hurry. "Sorry, gents. I'm a mite shellacked."

Fargo saw no weapons, and the man did indeed smell like a mash vat. "Mistaken identity," he told the drunk, watching him nevertheless even after he'd passed.

"Man alive," Wade complained. "This is a perfect city for killers to disappear in. Especially when you only know what one of them looks like."

"Straight-arrow," Fargo agreed. "We have two names now. More important, we know one of them is Tutt's cousin. I don't think Frank had anything to do with the killings, but he's holding back—we're going to force him to show his hole cards."

"Now?"

"Nah. That clean linen in the hotel room is calling my name."

Despite the hour, the hotel lobby was crowded. Fargo spotted the copper-haired woman named Constance, busy writing a letter, but no sign of the lovely Leora. The two men were heading toward the fancy spiral staircase when the tall clerk with the beanpole build called out diffidently: "Mr. Fargo?"

"Better stick with me, Wade," Fargo said in a low voice. "I still don't trust this chicken plucker."

They crossed to the big marble counter.

"Mr. Fargo," the clerk said in a confidential tone, "you gave me . . . strict orders not to give your room number to anyone."

"That order still stands."

"Oh, yessir! But you see, a certain young lady asked me for it, and I told her I couldn't give it out. She wanted to leave a note for you, so I took it. Here it is."

He handed Fargo a sheet of lavender stationery. The deckle-edged sheet had been folded and sealed with wax.

"Thanks," Fargo told him, slipping him four bits in silver.

He broke the seal and read the short message: *We were interrupted just as things got interesting. My father turns in early and sleeps soundly. I'm in room 311 if you'd care to . . . continue our discussion.*

There was no signature, but Fargo didn't need one. A fine golden hair had been enclosed. Only now did he notice Wade reading past his shoulder.

"You nosy pup, I ought to pop you on your snot locker."

"Holy mackerel!" the young officer blurted out. "A damn Greek goddess like Leora inviting you to her room—and this late! Man alive, Mr. Fargo! You just got done running one beauty out of town and the remount is saddled and ready."

Fargo couldn't suppress a grin at that remark. "Maybe you haven't noticed, but that gal Constance is eyeing you up like fresh fruit. I think you ought to bait that hook—she's a fast young lady, as they say back in the land of steady habits."

Wade sent a glance her way. "Yeah, maybe I will try my luck. You know, except for the buck teeth, I s'pose she's not so bad."

"All cats look alike in the dark," Fargo assured him. "Good hunting."

"If I was with Leora," Wade retorted as he pivoted on his heel to cross the lobby, "it wouldn't be in the dark. Not the way she looks."

Fargo enthusiastically agreed. He'd been with regal beauties and even a few homely lonelys, busy as a bee sampling flowers all over the land. But Leora Padgett rated aces high even among the most beautiful he'd ever sampled.

However, he still didn't trust that damn clerk. Fargo moved on cat feet down the third-floor hallway, his Colt to hand. When he reached the door of 311, he tapped it with the muzzle of the six-shooter, his head in constant motion to look both ways.

"Skye?" a low feminine voice called through the door.

"Yeah. Open the door, Leora, and then stand aside. I want to see the entire room."

Fargo didn't mistrust the girl, but she could have been forced into setting a trap for him. She did as instructed. Fargo saw a sumptuously appointed room even fancier than his, including a tester bed and a satinwood wardrobe. He even glanced behind the door, but no one was lurking.

He stepped inside and she closed and locked the door, turning to watch as he holstered his gun. She wore only a thin linen wrapper, her golden tresses tumbling loose.

"I suppose you think I'm shameless," she greeted him, her heart-shaped lips forming a little moue.

"I certainly hope you are," he replied, eyes taking her measure.

"Did you honestly think the Butcher Boys were up here?" she teased.

Fargo tossed his hat on a side chair and followed it with his gun belt. "I didn't come up here to talk about them. Or to talk. I came to see something."

"Such as . . . ?"

"Shuck out of that wrapper."

"Oh, you'd like to see this?"

The linen wrapper fell in a puddle at her feet. The sight made Fargo late for his next breath and sent a surge of blood into his man gland. She was delicately sculpted but with a perfect symmetry to her body. High, thrusting breasts flush in the ripeness of womanhood; a flat, flawless stomach that seemed poured from creamy lotion; hourglass hips; supple legs ending in perfectly turned ankles. And at the juncture of those legs, a perfect "V" of dark blond mons bush.

"Yeah," Fargo finally managed to reply. "That's what I had in mind."

"Now, you," she insisted "get naked as a jay."

Generally, Fargo left on as many clothes as possible when he took a woman. But this one had his blood singing with the urge to merge his flesh with hers. When he stepped out of his trousers and she spotted his curved saber, swollen purple at the tip, she stared like a bird mesmerized by a snake.

"My stars, Skye! I've seen a few of those, but . . . just looking at yours fills my mind with lustful thoughts. A wild tumble of them."

Fargo took a second, longer look at those hard, full tits with their perky strawberry nipples. "Yeah, I take your drift. But it's not fragile—you can touch it if you'd like."

"Oh, I'd *like*."

She took his hand and led him to the bed, assuming a take-charge manner as she pushed him onto it. He felt her hair tickling his stomach, her breath moist and animal-warm, as she took him in one hand and slowly stroked him while her playful tongue ran swirls around the sensitive tip. Soon Fargo's legs were twitching with uncontrollable pleasure— hot, tight, welling pleasure.

Fargo took over as lust drove him to enjoy this woman's body *now*. He rolled her onto the bed beside him and climbed into the saddle made by her splayed-out legs. She was long past ready for him, and he slipped in easily, his size parting her velvet tunnel and almost instantly coaxing a first, gasping climax from her.

She wasn't a talker or screamer, and Fargo liked that— especially with her father sleeping next door. Over and over he flexed his buttocks and rocked his hips, making sure both of them felt the pleasure in as many spots as possible. After a string of escalating climaxes, the grand seizure was on her, and Fargo felt fiery ant bits of delicious pain as she dug her fingernails deep into his rocketing ass.

Having taken her over the peak, Fargo, too, gave in to the insistent prickling in his groin, bucking powerfully as he finished. They both lay gasping, their breathing erratic for uncounted moments. Even longer, they lay quietly dazed, their muscles like water, their wills powerless, their minds devoid of thought.

Finally Fargo managed to sit up, then stand and put on his clothes and gun belt.

"Think we can do this again?" Leora asked, watching him from the bed and lazy as a French courtesan.

Fargo cast a final, long glance at her remarkable charms. "I sure's hell hope so, lady. But I've got some nasty work ahead and it's about time to force it to the fever crisis."

"The Butcher Boys, right?"

He smiled and touched his index finger to his lips. "Shush. I don't want to hear that name while I'm looking at you."

Fargo said good night and closed her door behind him. Then he returned to the room, where Wade was already snoring like a crosscut saw. Despite the pleasant visit in room 311, Fargo didn't drop off into a peaceful sleep. Instead, he drifted down a long tunnel into fitful slumber, hearing the obscene buzzing of thousands of flies in a feeding frenzy.

# 16

The four desperate men who had come to be known as the Butcher Boys knew they had a formidable enemy in Skye Fargo—an implacable enemy who did not have the word surrender in his vocabulary once he latched onto a spoor. They knew their only chance for survival was to follow strict discipline and, above all else, kill him before he killed them.

Toward that lethal end, they had stuck by the arrangement made when they rented a small lean-to room off the rear of Paddy's Tavern. Pairing up, only two men stayed in the room at one time while the other two tried to keep an eye on Fargo and his towhead companion. This precaution also prevented Frank Tutt's gunmen from airing all of them out, thus forcing Tutt to fear the serious threat contained in the tin box hidden outside of town. So long as the Butcher Boys had that box, they had an ally in the effort to feed Fargo to the worms.

On the morning following Fargo's pleasant tryst with Leora Padgett, Jed Longstreet and Ray Nearhood were holed up in the dingy lean-to with its rammed-earth floor, sharing a bottle of forty-rod.

"This goddamn Fargo is a hard man to kill," Nearhood complained, his raw-liver gums flashing when he tipped the bottle back for a jolt. "I hear that gun thrower Tutt hired use to ramrod a bunch of Border Ruffians back in Missouri. *Them* sumbitches eat their own guts and ask for seconds. But Fargo had him pissing down his leg before that hired gun showed the white feather."

Jed Longstreet nodded glumly. Both men were sprawled out on the two crude shakedowns that made up the room's furnishings along with a three-legged stool and a slop bucket.

"According to Baylis," Jed said, "ol' Tutt might be gettin'

chicken guts about killing Fargo. He thinks Fargo suspects that we're all in this together, and Tutt is scared spitless his name will get tied to ours."

Nearhood snorted, passing the bottle to his companion. "Yeah, and you can't hardly blame him. That bastard Baylis is plumb loco. Christ, what kind of sane man carves out a woman's innards and piles 'em on her breast?"

Longstreet nodded. "That's the kind of shit red savages do. But the fat is in the fire now, chappie. The law sees all four of us as the Butcher Boys, and we'll either hang together or escape together."

"That's the straight. If one of us is pinched, it will all come out from witnesses who seen us together."

Jed took another pull, shuddering as the potent mash exploded in his belly. "So the best chance is to kill Fargo and then hightail it out of this region. Once we're shut of this place, we can all split up for good."

"You're gettin' ahead of the roundup, Jed. Everything you just said is true. We can't pull foot until Fargo is cold as a wagon wheel. But saying ain't doing, and like I told you, he's one tough hombre to kill."

"It's more than just tough—the son of a bitch is smart as a steel trap. How long you think we can sit here before he finds us and papers the walls with our brains? Man, we *got* to figure out a play, and mighty damn quick."

Jed passed the bottle back. "Jumping him in the street just won't work. The crafty bastard has spent so long depending on his eyes out on the frontier that a man can't sneak up on him. Look what happened to Hiram, and he's a slippery little weasel. Hadn't been for that shit-for-brains sheriff interfering, we'd all four be maggot fodder."

"God's truth. And no way in hell can we plug him in that fancy hotel. Too many witnesses, and by now the desk clerk is so afraid of Fargo he won't help us even if we flay his soles."

"We'll have to keep checking liveries for Fargo's stallion. If—"

The flimsy door rattled under three sharp knocks. Both men paled and filled their hands.

"Yeah, who is it?" Nearhood called out.

"Sheriff Hank Kinkaid. I want to ask you some questions."

Jed lowered his voice to a whisper. "Should we kill him?"

Nearhood shook his head. "Tutt says he's a dumb galoot. Just stick to the stories we made up."

They leathered their shooters and Nearhood crossed to the door, turning the chunk of board that served as a lock. He pushed the door open and Kinkaid stepped inside, blocking the bright sunshine. He took a quick glance around the hovel, nose wrinkling at the stench from the slop pail.

"Who are you fellows?" he inquired.

"My name's Dooley Johnson," Nearhood replied. "That lanky cuss on the shakedown is Slappy Danford."

"Slappy?" Kinkaid repeated. "Mite queer for a front name, ain't it?"

"My real name is Stanley," Longstreet informed the lawman. "But I don't let that get out much."

The sheriff grunted at that. "You two boys here alone?"

"Well, we had a whore in here the other night," Nearhood said. "Other 'n that it's just us two."

"You can't be local fellows or I'd a seen you by now. Where you hail from?"

"I'm from up north in the Green River country," Longstreet lied. "And before we met, Slappy was cutting firewood for steamboats up on the Missouri."

"Ahuh. Well, no offense intended, but this ain't exactly the Astor House you're living in. Most people who bother to come all the way to Santa Fe can afford a room with a window. How'd you come to drift down here?"

Nearhood said, "We tried our luck panning for gold up in Cherry Creek. When we went bust, this feller told us the caravans making up for the King's Highway sometimes hire outriders. We're hoping to get on."

Kinkaid mulled all this and nodded. "Have you boys heard about this notorious gang of killers the newspapers call the Butcher Boys?"

Nearhood didn't miss a beat. "Hell, who hasn't?"

"There's a five-hundred-dollar reward on them. If you hear or see anything, while you're out and about, come to my office. It could end your money troubles."

Kinkaid left, and Nearhood watched his retreating back through a chink in the door.

"Jesus Christ and various saints," he swore. "If that big lummox is smart enough to go around knocking on doors, what's to stop Fargo?"

Longstreet nodded, his hatchet profile deeply troubled. "Yeah, and what if he comes while Hiram is here? Fargo has seen his face, and he won't likely forget them ugly pockmarks."

"Fargo ain't the kind to forget a damn thing. We got to palaver with Baylis and Hiram quick as we can. The net is tightening. We got to kill Fargo, sell that box back to Tutt, and light a shuck outta here, Jed."

"And we best be quicker than an Indian going to crap," Longstreet added. "That old man we killed in that shack near Chimayo was the closest thing Fargo had to a family, and Baylis carving on him like he done—and leaving that goddamn severed finger for Fargo to find—was consarn foolish. It's end it or mend it, and since we can't mend it, we damn straight better end it."

After another fancy-silverware breakfast at the hotel that left a gnawing of hunger in Fargo's stomach, he and Wade McKenna spent the better part of the morning perambulating the streets and numerous alleys of Santa Fe. Fargo spotted so many hard cases and down-at-the-heels drifters that his task seemed hopeless.

"I hate to say it," he told Wade as they emerged from a side street onto Calle Mayor, "but our best chance to spot these bastards is if they try to kill us again."

"We know what Hiram Steele looks like," Wade reminded him. "That's who I've been looking for."

"Same here. I noticed Sheriff Kinkaid knocking on doors in that shantytown at the end of Silver Street. That must mean the law dogs have no leads."

"Maybe we should try it."

Fargo waved the suggestion aside. "Kinkaid is a stubborn old coot, but that could get him shot. The Mountain Utes got a saying: 'Don't go looking for your own grave.' A door is a mighty dangerous thing when you don't know what's behind it."

"Yeah, like the lady or the tiger, right?"

"There's no difference between those two," Fargo opined as his sun-slitted eyes took the measure of the busy main street. "I'm worrying more about Corey's revolving-barrel shotgun. It was missing from his shack, and he would never have parted with it."

"You said it was an old flintlock relic."

"A Spanish six-pounder is an old relic, too, junior, but I once used one in Tucson to blow a mansion down around a slaver."

"Well, getting back to the subject of ladies," Wade probed as they walked north along the bustling boardwalk, "how did things go with Leora last night?"

"How'd they go with you and Constance?" Fargo countered.

"Ahh, she's all primer and no main charge. Dang near slapped me when I invited her up to the room for a belt."

Fargo's eyes stayed in constant motion even as a sardonic grin parted his face. "Jesus, kid, she ain't a sporting girl. She comes from the quality. You need to spout off some poetry or something to get them in the mood."

"Huh! Leora is way better quality than buckteeth. Did you spout poetry to *her*?"

"No," Fargo admitted. "But you're an innocent young lad. Women look at me and figure I'm the kind will risk buckshot in the ass as I leap out a window. They like that—adds a little savor to things."

"Yeah, it's your reputation," Wade decided. "But you earned it. Where we headed?"

"To see King Tutt. I want to find out more about this crater-face cousin of his."

"Yeah, I've been wondering about that," Wade said. "You really think Tutt is part of the Butcher Boys gang?"

"Nah. He doesn't have the stomach for their dirty deeds, and he's way too rich to mix with nickel-chasers. But those who hold a candle for the devil do the devil's work."

A tout, a kid of about twelve years of age, stood in front of the Gilded Cage enticing passersby.

"First drink's on the house, gents," he greeted them, giving each man a wooden token good for a drink. There were no slatted batwings here, just a set of carved double doors with a long oval of window in each door. Fargo was duly impressed when he pushed open a door and got his first glimpse of Tutt's gambling establishment.

No brass cuspidors here. Instead of the long, straight bar

with a brass footrail, common to saloons, Fargo saw a sleek, S-shaped bar of heavy teak with tall, comfortable chairs upholstered in red plush. The two bartenders wore suits and frilly white shirts with cravats. Much of the floor space was taken up by a pair of roulette wheels and green baize card tables. Paintings in gold scrollwork frames lined the walls.

"Holy Hanna!" Wade said in an awed voice. "It's even fancier than the hotel."

The patrons, Fargo noticed, were definitely of the upper crust. Rules of propriety were more relaxed in scandalous Santa Fe, where even "proper" women sometimes smoked and imbibed liquor in public establishments. Fargo spotted several eyeing him with curiosity—no doubt they'd never seen buckskins in this place before. If his presence bothered them, they hid it well.

Fargo ambled up to the bar and nodded at one of the bartenders. "Is Frank Tutt around?"

"No, sir," he replied in a civil tone. "I was just telling the major that Mr. Tutt is away on a business trip."

"The major?" Fargo craned his neck around just in time to see Major Bruce Harding headed for the door.

"Harding!" he called out.

The officer stopped and glanced toward the bar. It took him a few moments to recognize Wade McKenna standing beside Fargo. When he did, his dour face twisted into a scowl. He crossed to the two men in several long strides.

"Snap those heels together, Lieutenant! Why are you in mufti after I expressly forbade it?"

"Sir, I—that is, Mr. Fargo told me it would be better for our mission if—"

"I ordered him to," Fargo interceded matter-of-factly.

"I see, Lieutenant Colonel Fargo," the Major said sarcastically. "I must have missed the change-of-command ceremony."

Harding smoothed his mustache with a knuckle, staring at Fargo now. "If he's on some goddamn 'mission,' Fargo, what's he doing here?"

"Funny thing," Fargo said. "I was just wondering the same thing about you. Why would an army officer be looking for Frank Tutt?"

Harding didn't like the turn this conversation was taking.

He stormed out in high dudgeon, leaving Fargo to speculate with narrowed eyes.

"You know, shavetail," the Trailsman said as the two men headed back out into the sunny street, "lots of times when you turn a rock over, you'll find a slug underneath."

Before they could move far from the door, a familiar voice called out behind them: "Fargo, hold up a minute!"

Brad Matlock, the young gun tough who worked for Tutt, came outside to join them. He glanced around to make sure no one was listening.

"It ain't no business trip," he said. "Tutt is scared shitless and has gone into hiding."

"Scared of me?" Fargo said.

"Well, it sure's hell ain't the boogerman."

"Why? I'm not gunning for him, and I told him so."

Matlock lifted a shoulder. "Tutt ain't one to confide in his hirelings. All I know is, he's convinced you mean to snuff his wick. You or somebody else."

"There's only one reason he needs to be scared of me—if he's made common cause with the Butcher Boys. Has he?"

Matlock mulled that as if he hadn't considered it. "Now you mention it, there was a couple of rough-looking jaspers in to see him recently. They parleyed in his office, and when they was done, Frank looked a little green. Usually, after he swings a shady deal, he gets all cheerful and buys us boys a drink. Not this time."

Fargo said, "I don't quite take your drift."

"Well, it was more like whatever them two was up to, it left Frank acting nerve-jangled—like maybe he was trapped between the sap and the bark."

Fargo and Wade exchanged a quick glance.

"Did you know," Fargo asked the gun thrower, "that one of the Butcher Boys is Tutt's cousin, Hiram Steele?"

Matlock, who had taken out the makings to build a cigarette, looked up in what seemed to be genuine surprise. "No shit? I knew Frank had a worthless cousin name a Hiram, but he's fiddle-footed and I never seen him. Frank calls him a no-dick piker."

"Did one of the hombres you saw have a pockmarked face?"

"Looked like rats ate his face. Matter fact, *he* looked like a rat. Sneaky little eyes flickin' all over the damn place."

Fargo nodded. "That's Steele. So you got no idea where Tutt is or when he'll be back?"

"No, and I don't much give a sweet fuck-all. That prissy bastard pays good wages, all right, but he's one a them sweet-lavender nancy boys who talks down to men who keep his poncy-ass alive."

"I 'preciate your help," Fargo said. "Just one more question: Has Tutt still got the order out to kill me?"

Matlock snorted as he twisted both ends of his quirly. "After the way you gelded that peacock at the Black Cat? That was Colt Tipton, one a the most expensive gunslicks in the territory. Now nobody wants the job, and that includes me. I'd sooner tangle with a sore-tailed grizz."

Fargo had forgotten about Harding, but Wade spoke up. "Mr. Matlock, any idea why Major Harding was here looking for Tutt?"

Brad Matlock thumbed his hat back, looking at the young soldier as if he were a poodle that had just spoken. "Fargo, does this child's mother know where he is?"

Fargo didn't quite succeed at hiding his grin. "He's green wood, maybe, but it's solid grain clear through."

"If you say so. Well, sonny, to answer your question, Harding and Tutt have been talking chummy for at least a year now. Harding even sends him cases of liquor. But Tutt doesn't tell me a thing."

Just then Fargo noticed a face flash for a moment from the mouth of an alley across the wide street.

"Hell's a-poppin'!" he shouted to the other two. "Eat dirt!"

Fargo was about to drop with them when he realized a well-dressed matron had just stepped into the street, a small child in each hand. Cursing the luck, he dove after them even as a withering din of gunfire erupted from the alley. Matlock, seeing the problem, rose up to his knees and filled his hand, fanning the hammer to throw suppressing fire at the assailants.

Fargo hauled the woman down by her clothing, the kids toppling with her. "Stay down!" he barked at her, rolling hard and fast to join his friends.

Wade, despite the fact that his face was a mask of fear,

**134**

reacted like a soldier, bringing his Colt up and firing carefully spaced, carefully aimed shots. By now the main street of Santa Fe had erupted in screams of terror. Violence on Silver Street rarely even made the newspaper, but daylight gun battles in the middle of town were rare.

Fargo found little to aim at but tossed lead anyway. Matlock, perhaps to show off for the other two, had remained up on his knees. It was a lethal mistake—he was inserting his spare cylinder when Fargo heard an ugly, familiar noise like a hammer hitting a melon. Blood suddenly fountained from Matlock's forehead and a pebbly clot of brain matter spurted out the back of his skull. He folded forward and flopped into the dust, legs twitching a few times as his nervous system tried to deny the fact of death.

"Katy Christ!" Wade exclaimed, watching the man's blood pool rapidly in the dirt.

"Shoot through the wood of that harness shop!" Fargo ordered. "Right where the front and side walls come together! They're firing from there!"

Fargo had calculated correctly. Only moments after they concentrated their fire on that spot, all firing ceased from the alley. Even as he rose in pursuit, the drumming of escaping hooves reached his ears.

He looked at Matlock's sprawled body and felt something rare for him—a stab of guilt. It only intensified when he saw the woman and children crying in the street, afraid to move.

"This is my fault, kid," Fargo said. "I know he was an unsavory type, but I liked Matlock. He treated me with respect, and that gutsy play he made fanning his hammer might have saved me *and* that family."

The usual crowd was beginning to gather, staring at Matlock as if he were a freak on display.

"Your fault?" Wade said, thumbing reloads into his service revolver. "The Butcher Boys started this."

"Yeah, but I knew they were desperate. This attack in broad daylight shows just how desperate. We can't risk the citizens like this. You and me are heading out of town, and we're making damn sure this bunch knows it. And the next time we hug with those bastards, we're putting paid to it."

# 17

After that noisy and deadly shooting affray in the middle of Santa Fe, Fargo decided discretion was the better part of valor. He and Wade spent the next few hours in their hotel room playing joker poker and waiting for the inevitable knock on their door.

Around six p.m. it came.

"Would that be Sheriff Kinkaid?" Fargo called out, right hand on the butt of his Colt.

"It ain't the tooth fairy," replied a familiar gravelly voice.

Fargo nodded to Wade, who rose from the table to let the lawman in.

"Before you wind in to your spiel," Fargo greeted him, tossing down his cards, "I didn't start that little fracas today."

Kinkaid folded his arms and let out a fluming sigh. "Hell, I know that, Trailsman. I spoke to several witnesses, including the woman you pulled from the line of fire. You, the kid here, and Brad Matlock were all chewing the fat in front of the Gilded Cage when the shooters opened up on you."

"Matlock wasn't too smart that time," Fargo said, "but he's got guts. He exposed himself to a wall of lead to make sure I got the woman and her kids down. You might tell that to the ink slingers, for all the good it will do him."

"They already know. But damn it, Fargo, don't you see how it is? I understand how you feel about wanting to square things for your pard Corey Webster. That's how the whole town feels about the Sloan family, too. But Santa Fe ain't like some other towns on the frontier. So long as you're here, lead *will* fly, and now it's flying in the part that's usually safe for women and kids."

"Mm. And so you're here to run me out of town."

"It ain't me. Hell, I ain't never run a law-abiding man out of town. Matter fact, I generally don't run the criminals out if they mind their pints and quarts. But I ain't the big bushway around here—it's the mayor and the governor."

"Well wipe that hangdog look off your face, Sheriff. Me and the kid are pulling up stakes tomorrow morning."

Kinkaid's weather-seamed face brightened, if that were possible. "You are?"

Fargo nodded. "I came to that decision right after the shootout. But I don't want the Butcher Boys hearing that version of it. I want them to think I left town chasing after them."

Kinkaid's face was a mask of confusion. "That's too far north for me. How can you chase after them when we know they're in town?"

"Do you know who Leora Padgett is? That stunning young blonde who spends a lot of time writing letters in the lobby?"

"I don't know her the way you prob'ly do, but yeah, I know who you mean. She's hard to miss."

"Well, earlier today I had her write an anonymous letter to the newspaper. Perfumed stationery and all that. It claims she overheard me and Wade talking about how we got a tip that the Butcher Boys are holed up in Taos. I'll lay odds they light out after us—or even before—and try to kill us somewhere along the trail."

Kinkaid mulled that. "Hell, while you're headed north they could just light a shuck in some other direction—Mexico, San Francisco, maybe back east."

"I don't think they have the money yet. I think they were counting on Tutt for that, and he's crawled into a hole somewhere."

Kinkaid's jaw went slack. "Tutt? He's in cahoots with a bunch like that?"

"I can't exactly prove that. I think it's more like they're putting the squeeze on him over something. Even if they could dust their hocks out of here, I think they realize I'm not letting this go. I'll follow them to the moon."

Kinkaid pulled at the end of his chin, digesting all of this. "So you leave and the Butcher Boys go with you. And of course, if they're trying to douse your light, you have every right to fight back."

"So the mayor and the governor get what they want, and you law dogs have no beef with me."

"It ain't quite that neat, Fargo. It leaves me looking like a laughingstock. A well-liked local family is rubbed out, butchered like hogs, and it takes the famous outsider Fargo to settle accounts. I'd call that a beef."

Fargo's voice hardened. "This ain't some goddamn petty pissing contest between me and you. You just said it: butchered like hogs. You think I'm after jewels in paradise? You saw those women, Kinkaid. You saw their faces, how the pain was etched in deep. You talk about trials and such—mad dogs like that need to be cut down on sight."

*"Ley fuga,"* Kinkaid said, nodding agreement.

*"Ley fuga,"* Fargo agreed.

"Flight law," Wade translated, knowing some Spanish. "What's that?"

"An old Mexican custom," Kinkaid explained. "When lawmen down there caught the worst criminals far from civilization, they just shot them in the back and claimed they tried to flee. It saved the cost of a trial and execution."

"Only, this time," Fargo promised, "the bullet holes will be in the front."

The *Santa Fe New Mexican* published twice a day, an early-morning "bulldog" edition and an abbreviated late-afternoon broadside version that plastered the most sensational stories on walls all over the city. When Fargo and Wade went into the street, on the morning after Kinkaid's visit, Fargo's lips eased into a grin.

"Leora did good work," he said, nodding to a broadside on the front of the hotel. "It came out last night."

Wade read the headline aloud: "'Skye Fargo Pursues Butcher Boys to Taos Hideout.'"

Both men quickly read the brief teaser intended to sell that morning's edition.

"It doesn't even mention me," Wade complained.

"You want a sugar tit to comfort you?" Fargo barbed. "The point is that the killers most likely saw it. And since it's always

**138**

better to be ahead of your quarry than behind him, I'd wager they're already on their way."

"How will they know which way we'll ride?"

"Lieutenant, this isn't Massachusetts. Thanks to those mountains you see to the northeast, there's only one trail to Taos. It follows the Rio Grande and skirts the Sangre de Cristo Range on their west side."

They headed toward Manuel's livery. Wade seemed worried about something.

"What's bitin' at you?" Fargo demanded.

"It's just—this business with letting them get ahead of us and take up ambush positions. It runs counter to smart military strategy."

"Oh, it's hindside foremost, all right. Usually you don't want your enemy to spot your hand before you play it. But these four are pure pus, and we have to draw them out."

Wade nodded. "I take your drift. Being criminals, and cowards, they might not come after us because they'd have to brace us on the trail. This way they can dry-gulch us and not have to show themselves."

At the livery they tacked their mounts and squared their livery bill. Fargo checked his saddle panniers for supplies. "We've got plenty of jerked buffalo and a double handful of raisins. And one airtight of tomatoes. How's your larder?"

"I've still got the hardtack they gave me at the fort, but it's got weevils in it."

"We'll just make bully soup out of it."

"The heck is that?" Wade asked as they led their mounts out into the hoof-packed yard.

"You just soak it in coffee. That way it won't break your teeth and the weevils float to the top."

Hoping the Butcher Boys had taken Fargo's bait, the two men tilted their hats against the early sun and rode northeast out of Santa Fe. Just in case the killers had gotten a late start, Fargo held to an easy pace so the gang could swing wide around them.

The first leg of the trail was easy terrain, rolling hills covered with scrub pine and juniper with the occasional thickly wooded hollow.

"Don't forget," Fargo said at one point. "It's most likely

they'll wait until the rugged country to open up on us—it's easier to hide if they miss. But this kind are lazy bastards, and they might drop a bead on us at any time. Watch your horse's ears close—they'll prick forward if he picks up the man smell. This stallion has saved me many a time."

By late morning the trail was rising and the horses starting to blow. Fargo called a halt and they watered them from their hats using the goatskin of water lashed to Fargo's saddle fender.

"Damn, that's pretty country," Wade remarked, gazing off to their west. They had a good view of the Rio Grande, reflecting like burnished gold in the sunlight. Local Pueblos worked the patchwork quilt of chili pepper and bean fields in the river valley.

"Mighty pretty," Fargo agreed. "Those Indians were working those fields long before anybody ever heard of Valley Forge. Matter fact, I can remember a time when I rode from El Paso to Canada and never saw a soldier, a miner, or a house except for a tipi. Now the West is peopling up and it won't be long before a man won't have room to swing a cat in."

"The Good Lord must've put it here for us to use," Wade reasoned.

"The Good Lord ain't my department, soldier blue," Fargo said. "But do you think the Good Lord wants men to wash away the Sierras with giant hoses called dictators just to scratch out more gold than we need? Does He want all the trees felled so men can make telegraph poles and railroad ties? I don't begrudge any man his living, but I've seen those filthy cities back in the States, and I'm damned if I want to see more out here."

"Well, when you put it that way," Wade replied as they swung up into leather and resumed their trek, "it's hard to gainsay you."

The next time Wade tried to start a conversation Fargo put the kibosh on it. "Tamp down the flap-jaw, kid. Keep your mind on both sides of the trail. There's boulders and cutbanks now all around us. Watch for reflections and any sudden flights by birds."

Tensed for action as they were, both men flinched in the saddle when a puma suddenly darted across the trail. The

Ovaro took it in stride, but Wade's cavalry sorrel nickered and crow-hopped, fighting the reins. But West Point rated high in horsemanship, and Wade expertly calmed the animal.

"Does *any*thing bother that Ovaro of yours?" Wade marveled.

"Bears can throw him into a panic, and once he tossed me ass over applecart when a damn rabbit shot across the trail. But he's bullet savvy and never spooks in a shootout."

Fargo kept his sun-crimped eyes in motion as he said this, watching everything. Some rough weather was coming, all right, sunny day or no. These Butcher Boys knew they could never draw an easy breath while he was alive, and desperation usually made men crazy brave.

An hour later, with the sun now westering, they rode into the ancient Nambe Pueblo, a scattering of small adobe dwellings with outdoor ovens. A few men tended flocks of sheep on the slope leading down to the river. A moonfaced *indio* woman selling tamales wrapped in corn husks flashed them a gap-toothed grin.

"Drink," she invited them, pointing to the rain barrel at the corner of her house. Both men accepted her offer, dismounting and tanking up on the cool water.

"Might's well buy some of them tamales," Fargo said. "Beats the hell out of bully soup."

Two small children were playing a hoop-and-stick game nearby. The woman said something in rapid Spanish and they scuttled into the house. Although the woman seemed cordial enough, Fargo noticed a distant, wary look in her eyes—eyes that seldom made contact with his for fear he would steal her soul.

And just maybe, he thought, the last whiteskins to ride through here hadn't been all that friendly.

Fargo handed her some coins and placed the food in some cheesecloth he carried in his pannier. "Wade," he said, "you claim to palaver Spanish good. Ask this lady if four horse-backers passed this way recently—white men."

*"Senora, ha visto usted cuatro hombres en caballo? Hombres blancos?"*

Those distant eyes suddenly turned into two dead buttons and she averted her gaze.

"She understood me," Wade insisted. "She—"

"Let it go," Fargo said. "She's scared, and why shouldn't she be? All outsiders have ever brought to these remote villages is death, disease, and misery."

As they were riding out, Wade said, "I don't get it. She told those two kids in Spanish to go into the house. But she told the one closest to her to tell 'that one' to go with him. She meant the other kid, but why didn't she say his name?"

"They won't use their names in front of whites. They figure their names have power but lose it if a white man hears it pronounced."

"They seem like nice enough people, but they're sure superstitious."

"I s'pose, but you ought to see them laugh when they're told that a virgin had a baby."

But Fargo's mind wasn't on the conversation. "You know," he said, "if that woman had *not* seen any white riders, she most likely would've just said no. But she just sewed up her lips."

"So you think the Butcher Boys did ride through?"

"The flocks have covered over any tracks," Fargo replied, loosening his Henry in its scabbard. "But they're out there waiting for us, soldier blue. Sure as gumption they're out there."

# 18

"Here they come, boys," Baylis Ulrick announced. "Fargo and that snot-nosed kid siding him. Maybe two miles distant and closing at an easy trot."

He lowered his field glasses quickly to avoid telltale reflections. The four men occupied the crown of a large boulder about thirty yards back from the narrow Taos Trail.

"Fargo!" Jed Longstreet spat the word out of his mouth as if it were a bad taste. "Wasn't for that crusading son of a bitch, we coulda just hung around Santa Fe milking Hiram's cousin for running-around money. But Fargo turned his liver white and made Tutt rabbit. And I 'spect we ain't gonna see Tutt again until Fargo either lights a shuck outta this territory or we let daylight into him."

Hiram Steele made a farting noise with his lips. "Fargo, light a shuck before he kills us? You gotta be shitting us, Jed. That mother-loving bastard ain't the kind to swim half a river. He's *for* us now, and we best kill him first or he turns all four of us into worm castles."

"Hiram is an ugly little runt," Baylis put in, "but he's right as rain. Once Fargo's planted we're on Fiddler's Green. We can even go back to Santa Fe and put the squeeze on Tutt. Sheriff Kinkaid talks tough, but he's old and stupid—couldn't locate his own ass at high noon in a hall of mirrors."

Baylis paused to study the terrain around them. Since riding out of that raggedy-ass Indian pueblo, they had avoided coulees and defiles whenever possible, sticking to the high ground just behind the rimrock to the right of the trail. It was slower going, but kept them out of Fargo's gunsights.

"We need to make a play," he said, "and it will have to be

down here. Close in, where a man ain't likely to miss. One shot that wipes Fargo out of the saddle."

"Two, you mean," Ray Nearhood corrected him. "That green antler with him is a soldier, don't forget."

Baylis snorted. "A soldier is just a boy with his pants tucked into his boots. Sure, we'll kill him, too, but it's Fargo we have to worry about. But don't nobody get any damn fool notions about pulling down on him in a draw-shoot. They say that lanky bastard can *magic* a gun into his hand."

"While we jack our jaws," Nearhood fretted, "them two are riding closer. How do we play this thing?"

"*We* don't," Baylis said. "See that mulberry thicket on the other side of the trail? It's small but it's perfect cover for one man. Any more will risk exposure—Fargo's got the eyes of a hawk. The rest of us take all the horses back up to the rimrock on this side of the trail and wait."

The other three Butcher Boys exchanged frowning glances at this plan.

"One of us?" Hiram repeatedly skeptically. "Baylis, is your garret furnished? This is Skye goddamn Fargo, not that shit-for-brains rancher we done for outside of Santa Fe."

"Damn straight," Longstreet chimed in. "And *which* one of us?"

Ulrick's mouth twisted into a scornful smirk. "Maybe you *ladies* best stick your hands down your pants, see if you own a pair. We'll draw lots. And what's so loco about the plan? Fargo will be looking for all four of us to jump him, so that tiny thicket won't even catch his notice."

Nearhood nodded, swinging toward the plan. "Baylis is right, boys. Hell, what's so great about Fargo? He couldn't even locate us in Santa Fe, and every time he peddled lead at us, he missed. Looks to me like he spent more time gettin' pussy than he did beatin' the tall weeds after us."

This drew laughter from the other three, and Baylis thumped his back. "Well said, green teeth. Jerk a weed loose and turn around. Tear it into four pieces."

"Look here, Baylis," Hiram said nervously. He nodded toward the formidable four-barrel shotgun with the revolving barrels. It protruded from his saddle boot. "Whoever draws short lot, can't he at least take the crowd leveler into that thicket with him?"

Baylis shook his head. "Use your think piece, man. No long guns in that thicket. The second one of us brings the barrel down, it will stick out. No sir, it's short guns. We all got Sam Colt's finest, and they're deadly accurate out to forty feet. Fargo is riding on the left, and he'll be no more than ten feet away when the shooting commences. Plug him, then plug the snot nose."

Nearhood turned around with four pieces of weed sticking out of his hand. "All right, boys—let's draw lots."

Fargo reined in the Ovaro and swung down, squatting in the trail.

"A few old prints," he told Wade, "but the edges are starting to crumble. And a mule went through here a few hours ago, probably carrying a load of wood judging from how deep the hind tracks are. But our four friends left the trail some time back. The slope between here and the river is too exposed, so they must have taken to the high ground above us."

Wade cast a nervous glance above him. "Why? An ambush?"

Fargo forked leather again and gigged the Ovaro forward. "Could be. But they'd have to stay pretty high up to avoid detection, and I doubt this bunch are sharpshooters. It's more likely they left the trail to make us think we're safe down here."

"So you figure an attack is coming?"

"Well, they didn't make this ride to have a picnic."

Wade glanced at Fargo. "Jesus, are you grinning?"

"What's wrong with a man enjoying his work?"

Fargo's eyes swept the terrain. Boulders were scattered along the right side of the trail, the occasional tree or thicket along the left. It did not, however, appear to be the best dry-gulching area.

"Just keep your eyes peeled," he told his companion. "Watch your horse's ears. When the fandango comes, stay frosty and shoot plumb."

The ground cover cleared out for a moment on their left, and they saw a new fort with loopholed gun towers and squared-off walls of cottonwood logs going up down in the river valley.

"Fort Stanton," Fargo said. "Headquarters for the new Apache-fighting regiments."

"That's where I'd rather be than playing barber's clerk for Major Harding," Wade said wistfully.

"You just might end up there," Fargo said mysteriously. "I got me a gut hunch that Harding and Tutt might be moving to the calaboose soon."

When Wade pressed him on this matter, however, Fargo waved him silent. "No more chin music. Trouble's coming soon."

They covered perhaps another mile in silence, the only sounds the low squeaking of their saddles and the metallic chink of their bit rings. Fargo felt a familiar prickling on the back of his neck and pulled his Henry from its scabbard, balancing the butt plate on his right thigh. So far, though, he could detect nothing dangerous, and the Ovaro showed no signs of trouble.

It was Fargo's hawklike vision that picked up the clue. As they rounded the shoulder of a mountain he caught a quick glint in the corner of his left eye—it came from a small thicket just to the left of the trail. The kind of glint a gun barrel might reflect when the bluing had worn off.

*So that's what's on the spit,* Fargo thought.

Fargo reined in and Wade followed suit. Pretending to drink from his canteen, Fargo muttered from the side of his mouth: "I think this is the fandango. Get your carbine out and watch the high ground above us. The second you hear me busting caps, open fire above. Don't worry about targets. Just empty your magazine into the boulders and let the ricochets keep them hunkered down."

Wade nodded, knuckling his new hat back to clear his vision. Fargo gigged his stallion forward even as he brought the long barrel of the Henry down to the level. Without warning he dropped the reins and, working the lever rapidly, pumped six rounds into the thicket. Wade's hard-hitting Spencer tossed all seven rounds up into the rocks, where they whined from boulder to boulder.

There was a surprised grunt from the thicket followed by a heavy crashing noise. Wade thumbed reloads into the loading trap in the Spencer's butt and covered the high ground while Fargo swung down, Henry still aimed at the thicket. He reached inside, grabbed a handful of bloody shirt, and heaved the dead man into the trail.

"It's Crater Face," he announced, recognizing Hiram Steele. His left eye was now a bloody crater, and his lower jaw had been shot off. Brain blood still spumed from the eye wound, a bright red blossom. Fargo pulled him even farther onto the trail so the carrion birds and coyotes would have an easier time of it.

"Hallelujah!" Wade said. "You finally sent one under, Skye—uhh, I mean Mr. Fargo."

"Just call me Fargo now, Lieutenant, but remember we ain't swapping spit. And don't let this kill get you all giddy. Matter fact, you best understand it's getting down to the nut cutting now. And with Baylis Ulrick, master butcher, in the mix, that's not just a way of speaking. I won't blame you one bit if you throw in your hand."

"You don't think I have the sand to stick it out?"

Fargo stared at the ugly corpse at his feet. "The sand? Why, Christ, you're a West Point man. You'd harrow hell with an empty carbine. But there's a good chance you won't ride back from this one. These filthy jackals may have poor trail craft, but they're some pumpkins as murderers."

"All the more reason for me to stick. The law won't touch this bunch, and I took an oath to defend my fellow Americans from all enemies, foreign and domestic. Wouldn't you call this bunch domestic enemies?"

"Among other things," Fargo replied.

"All right then. Far as getting killed—it's a brevet or a coffin for *this* pony soldier."

Fargo grinned as he booted his Henry and swung up into leather. "There'll be no brevet for you and likely no coffin—just a nameless grave. But you're a crazy young son of a bitch, and I admire that in a man. Let's make tracks."

However, Fargo thought of something and lit down again. He returned to the thicket and selected a long, thin branch, using the Arkansas toothpick in his boot sheath to saw it loose. He sharpened both ends, then turned to the corpse.

"Turn your head, Wade, if you're squeamish," he warned.

"What are you doing?"

"There's a good chance those other three yellow curs are up there watching us with spyglasses. I figure turnabout is fair play."

Fargo carried a captured Cheyenne war hatchet in his saddlebag. He dug it out and made short work of severing Steele's head from his neck. He crammed one end of the sharpened stake into the neck stump, then anchored the grisly mess in the trail with the pain-contorted face staring up toward the rimrock.

"There," Fargo said as he mounted again. "I'm not one to mutilate the dead, but I want this bunch to see what happens once a man loses his head."

# 19

Jed Longstreet took a turn with the spyglasses, his face twisting in fear and disgust. "Jesus Christ with a wooden dick! That Fargo is crazy-by-thunder! Old Hiram looks like one a them puppet heads on a stick."

"He cut his goddamn head off," Ray Nearhood said. "I ain't seen nobody do shit like that but Comanches."

Baylis Ulrick gave a harsh bark of scornful laughter. "No? What about the Butcher Boys? I s'pose we leave sweet lavender on the ones we kill?"

"That butchering was all your doing," Nearhood retorted. "And that's how's come we got that goddamn bulldog Fargo nipping at our asses right now."

"The hell? You think I done it to ruffle his feathers? Fargo woulda dogged us no matter how we left the old man's body," Baylis said.

"Maybe so," Jed said, lowering the glasses. "But he wouldn't be chopping off no damn heads."

"Christ, why'n't you two take up sewing?" Baylis scoffed. "The hell's it matter what happens to a body after it's dead? You think they stay pretty in the grave? Worms and maggots turn it into greasy stew."

"Hiram wasn't easy to look at," Jed put in, "but he wasn't a bad sort."

"Piss on the little rodent," Baylis said. "He drew the short lot, and he was too damn slow. I ain't sorry he's dead. When we get that money from his cousin, now we only got to split it three shares. 'Course, if all this is too rich for your bellies, cut loose now. I ain't trying to sell nobody a bill of goods."

This appeal to greed calmed his two companions somewhat.

"Yeah, but with Hiram dead, will Tutt cough up the gelt?" Nearhood wondered.

Baylis lifted his chin in the direction of his horse. "You forget we got that little tin box in my saddlebag. He'll pay or he'll go to federal prison."

"What about Fargo?" Longstreet fretted, watching the two men below on the trail. "Ain't you noticed, Baylis? That son of a bitch ain't trying to catch us—he's deliberately poking along so we can get ahead of him. He *wants* us to try and kill him."

"Listen, both of you. This ain't no time to get the fantods, chappies. That's how Fargo works—he takes the nerve out of a man, then he strikes. It only works if you let it. I got a better plan than this last one. Straight arrow."

"I ain't goin' along with nothing," Nearhood protested, "iffen it means drawing lots again. We got to stay together."

"I was wrong to send one man," Baylis admitted. "But there's plenty of ways to kill a man, and not all of 'em requires tossin' lead. Grab leather, boys. Long as Fargo is letting us get ahead of him, let's oblige him."

By late afternoon the sun was a dull yellow orb sinking toward the horizon. The two horsebackers, alert for the ever-expected attack, climbed higher and higher into the foothills of the Sangre de Cristo Range, feeling the air cool and thin out. The Rio Grande was a muddy brown ribbon far below in the valley to their left, following a serpentine course through well-cultivated fields.

"Where in tarnal hell *are* they?" Wade wondered aloud, breaking a long silence. "Maybe that little show you put on with Steele spooked them off?"

"Not likely. This bunch is desperate."

"Think they're close?"

Fargo nodded. "Might even be within hailing distance."

Wade cocked his head with sudden interest. "You sound pretty sure. Have you seen sign?"

"Not lately. But if one oak bears acorns, all oaks will. Mad-dog killers run to type. And it's a type I've locked horns with plenty of times."

"Yeah, that makes sense," Wade said, craning his neck to study the rock-strewn slope to their right. It blocked their view of the snowcapped mountains to the east. "It's old hat for you, but this is all pretty new to me."

"You mistook my meaning," Fargo said. "I know the type and how they think. But I can't predict exactly where, when, or how they'll make their play. They might try another ambush on the trail. But they also know we'll have to make a camp—this trail is too narrow for night riding."

"So they might try to jump us in camp instead of mounting another ambush?"

"Yeah, or they might try both. Most criminals are stupid, but plenty of them are also cunning."

For a few minutes the steep slope on their right was split by a defile, and with his field glasses Fargo got an excellent view in every direction. To the northeast he could just see the adobe garrison at Taos, the only spot in America where the Stars and Stripes flew day and night by Congressional decree. Kit Carson's legendary stand had ensured that.

Between Fargo's present position and Taos rose the area's most famous landmark: two gigantic mounds of gray rock called *Huajatolla* by locals, Breasts of the World—or the Spanish Peaks as they were called in front of people who bathed often and used silverware.

"God-in-whirlwinds!" Wade exclaimed. "Those things must work on a traveler's mind when he's coming into Taos."

Fargo's strong white teeth flashed through his beard. "Yeah. The soiled doves do a lively trade in Taos."

"Not with Skye Fargo," Wade teased him. "He doesn't pay for it."

"It's nothing personal. I just don't believe in paying for something that's a man's natural right. And I prefer volunteers. The moans aren't rehearsed."

"I've never been to a sporting gal," Wade admitted. "The only woman I ever was with didn't moan—she told me to get the hell off her hair."

Fargo chuckled. "Son, you need some lessons in female geography."

When Wade tried to say something else, Fargo raised a hand. "Both of us are letting our tongues swing way too loose. Stop talking, stop thinking about women, and pay attention. We could ride into a shit-storm at any second."

Soon the imposing slope of boulders resumed on their right. Fargo, who had been studying the ground closely, suddenly reined in. He tossed the reins forward and swung down, kneeling just to the right of Wade's sorrel.

"Prints made by hobnail boots," he told Wade. "Same prints I found around Corey's shack. These are fresh."

"Just the one set? I don't see any tracks from horses."

"Nah. Just one man came down from the rimrock."

Wade pulled his carbine from the scabbard and looked around nervously. "Why?"

Fargo stood back up and slapped the dust off his hat. "That's a poser. Most likely he came down to study the trail closer, with an ambush in mind. But the slope on the left is free of cover right here, and there's no ground boulders on the right. So what was the point?"

However, another possibility had occurred to Fargo. For the past mile or so the trail had been narrowing as the left slope became steeper. By now the trail was only ten feet wide and he and Wade had been forced to ride single file.

"If they were to open fire on us from somewhere above," he speculated, "I mean really pour it to us, we'd have no room to maneuver out of the weather—not even to wheel and retreat. And if gunfire spooked our horses, there's a good chance they'd tumble down the left slope—it's a good three-hundred-foot drop and neither man nor horse would survive."

Wade let out a deep breath. "Doesn't sound like we have many options."

Fargo hit leather again and took up the reins. "I plan to enjoy my breakfast tomorrow, options be damned."

Despite his bravado, however, Fargo had begun to worry about another danger from above. But he was sick and tired of chasing this gang's dust and, come hell or high water, it was time to bring things to a boil. He didn't want to say too much to McKenna, though, because the young soldier was nervous enough.

"Listen," he said over his shoulder, "I want you to tighten your reins good so you've got control of your horse's head. If any ruckus starts up above us, *don't* let that sorrel look up. Hold his head level and just sink steel into his flanks. Don't even look yourself—if I give the whoop, just follow me at a two-twenty clip, y'unnerstan'? Take off like a scalded dog and don't rein in until I do."

Wade, assuming Fargo meant gunfire when he said "ruckus," replied, "Understood."

They rode perhaps another half mile, the trail growing from ten feet wide to eight. That prickle like lice crawling through his scalp was back, and Fargo was on the verge of picking up the pace when a low mutter like distant thunder sounded from above.

"Here she comes with a bone in her teeth!" he shouted. "Move it or lose it!"

Fargo didn't have to gig the trail-savvy Ovaro up—his master's trouble tone was all the spur he needed. But within a few heartbeats trouble was happening ten ways a second. The distant thunder rapidly grew closer on the steep slope, and when Fargo glanced up he felt his face go clammy—a huge wall of boulders, and a giant billow of dust, were bearing down on the trail like the last ding-dong of doom.

Already the first smaller rocks were splatting around them like giant buckshot, hurling so fast they were potentially deadly. Fargo pivoted in the saddle and loosed a curse when he saw that Wade's cavalry sorrel was bucking, not riding. The soldier was hanging on like a tick, but the horse was in a welter of fright and refusing to cooperate.

Then Wade made a smart play. He pulled a spare shirt from a saddle pannier and draped it over the sorrel's eyes. It calmed down immediately and lunged forward even as the first huge boulders crashed into the trail and then bounced down the cliff just to their left.

But Fargo feared the delay might have been enough to leave both men a soupy paste on the trail. Dust from the slope was now so thick it blinded and choked men and horses, and more and more juggernauts of death—some the size of steamer trunks—catapulted down around them. The entire slope above them seemed like a living, trembling beast shaking itself awake. The noise alone was enough to unstring a man's nerves.

Each man was on his own now. A rock punched into the Ovaro's neck hard, making him stumble, and when he staggered toward the drop-off, Fargo stood up in the stirrups, ready to save himself if the pinto went over. But the stalwart beast recovered and raced forward, unable to see the trail and guided by superior instinct and reflexes.

Fargo tried to make himself small in the saddle, expecting black oblivion with each blink of his eyes. But his wheel of fortune took an upward turn that day—they burst out of the chaotic dust cloud and Fargo found himself on a clear trail, the rock slide behind him.

But when he twisted around in the saddle to check on Wade, he felt his blood ice in his veins.

Wade and the sorrel had narrowly cleared the slide. But the dust-blinded sorrel had lost its footing, and now both rear legs hung over the lip of the cliff. Even as Fargo watched, the gelding was slipping farther over.

"Jump clear!" Fargo shouted to the beleaguered, whey-faced towhead.

"I can't! My right leg's pinned and he's dragging me with him!"

Fargo grabbed his lariat from the saddle horn, hoping to at least save Wade if not the sorrel. But when he looked at the horse, he realized there wasn't enough time. When a horse rolled its eyes like that, showing all whites, it was too panicked to do anything practical. And its bit was dripping foam, a sure sign it couldn't last more than a few seconds longer.

Fargo didn't waste another second. He lunged forward, bent over the sorrel's head, and took its left ear into his mouth. He bit down hard, hard enough to draw salty blood, then leaped back out of the way.

Fargo had learned a fine point about horses from observing the Northern Cheyenne warriors—the only emotion that could quickly overcome fear was anger. The sorrel whickered in fury, scraped its way to its feet, and promptly bucked Wade into the trail in an ungainly heap. Then the sorrel stood there trembling with anger.

"You okay?" Fargo asked, helping the shaken officer to his feet.

"My ass is sore, but I'm alive," the grateful shavetail said. "You saved my life, Mr. Fargo."

"Fargo, remember?"

Wade shook his head stubbornly. "Nope. We're back to Mr. Fargo now—you saved my doggone life just now!"

"Yeah, but that doesn't mean—"

"That we're swapping spit," Wade finished for him. "Man, I will not forget that biting-the-ear trick."

Fargo grinned. "Yeah, but neither will your horse. He thinks you bit him, and first chance he gets, he'll take a chunk out of your sitter. That's what mine did to me after I bit his ear. They *do* carry a grudge until it hollers mama."

Fargo glanced up the slope. "Well, the Butcher Boys almost doused our lights that time. Soon as your horse calms down, let's get the hell out of here. Night's coming on, and the terrain changes just ahead. We'll make camp and see who comes to visit us."

# 20

Fargo's prodigious skill at making memory maps proved right: Soon after they cleared the rock slide the terrain changed dramatically. The steep, rocky slope on their right gave way to a thickly forested ridge. With the sun now shimmering dully as it set in the west, they quickly scouted out a campsite.

Fargo chose a thick stand of wind-twisted juniper that formed a windbreak near a cold seep spring.

"Cold camp, right?" Wade asked.

Fargo shook his head. "Nope. That's why I chose this spot. It'll permit a good-size fire but provide a natural bulwark against a sudden attack. See all the rocks and boulders lying around? You can't rush this place—only sneak up on it."

"But a fire will mark us right out."

Fargo grinned. "Yeah, it will, won't it?"

After a brief hesitation, Wade grinned back. "Yeah, I just twigged the game."

"Best way to cure a boil—"

"Is to lance it."

Fargo looked pious. "Amen, Brother Wade."

The men drank deeply from the spring, then filled their canteens and let the horses drink. They stripped the leather from them, rubbed them down quickly, then strapped nose bags filled with oats on both mounts before hobbling them inside a nearby thicket, out of harm's way.

"Tonight," Fargo said as they softened bed ground with their knives, "you get to sleep in a Santa Fe bed."

"The hell's a Santa Fe bed?"

"You sleep on your belly and cover yourself with your back."

Wade groaned. "I'm popping a rib laughing." After a nervous pause he added: "I hear rattlesnakes are thick in this area?"

"Timber rattlers, yeah. If one curls up with you in the night, keep it warm until breakfast—it's good, tender meat."

"I'm a tenderfoot," Wade said good-naturedly, "and I deserve all this roweling."

"The rate you're going, you won't be a tenderfoot much longer. Matter fact, you're a good man to ride the river with."

"Careful, Mr. Fargo—you're close to slopping over."

Despite all this inconsequential banter, both men kept their eyes in motion as the grainy twilight of early evening settled over their camp. Fargo used handfuls of crumbled bark from his saddlebags and a sulfur match to start a fire in a circle of rocks. He laid the fire Indian style, burning the logs from the ends not the middle to avoid wasting wood.

Nights were cool at this elevation and the two men enjoyed the warmth of the flames as they split a can of tomatoes and strips of jerked buffalo meat. Fargo slid a thin Mexican cigar from his pocket and lit it with a piece of glowing wood. Now and then sparks rose in a thin column like fireflies.

"You expect trouble soon?" Wade asked quietly.

"Nah. They'll wait until we turn in. These boys don't cotton to showdowns—every attempt to kill us has been from ambush. They plan to plug us in our sleep."

"So we'll do turnabout on guard?"

Fargo blew twin streams of smoke out his nose. "Nope. We'll both turn in together and let them kill us."

Wade knew Fargo well enough by now to know that something was in the wind, so all he did was chuckle. Fargo didn't like to be pestered—he'd show his cards in good time.

"They could be watching us right now," was all Wade said.

"Prob'ly. But they're not close enough to use Corey's revolving-barrel shotgun yet—they're piss-poor shots with rifles and handguns, but they know that old flintlock won't need aiming, just pointing."

"These aren't men—they're animals."

"Like the lovely Rosita said, you're insulting the animal kingdom. Very few animals kill for pure sport."

While they spoke quietly Fargo sharpened his Arkansas toothpick against a flat stone, spitting on the stone now and then. Then he began sharpening four sticks into pointed stakes.

"What are those for?" a curious Wade asked.

"Just whittling," Fargo replied evasively.

"Uh-hunh. You're not the whittling type."

"Stop looking into that fire," Fargo admonished Wade. "It'll ruin your night vision. Listen, the two of us are going to gather up leaves and grass and make it look like we're putting it under our blanket rolls. While you're at it, pull a shirt and pants out of your saddlebags. They'll think we just want them to wear tomorrow morning."

"Don't we?"

Fargo shook his head as he pushed to his feet. "Nope. I'm going to show you a little ruse called the buckskin man."

Soon the two men had returned to the fire, which Fargo had deliberately let burn down to cover their next action. Both men stuffed their spare clothing to fill them out in the crude shape of men. Next they laid them out clearly on the bedrolls, even balancing their hats as if covering their faces in slumber.

"All right," Fargo whispered, "here's the chancy part. You go hide in that clutch of boulders near the spring. Then I'll roll a couple big pieces of wood onto the fire and join you. When it burns hot, they'll have a good view of us and think we're crapped out for the night."

"Think they'll strike quick?"

"Soon enough. They'll want some firelight on us."

Wade rose up, a grin twitching at his lips. "You've got a trick for every occasion, haven't you?"

"Damn near, but they don't always work. Just haul your freight into those boulders and keep your head down. Don't look into the fire and check the action on your revolver. Remember—these graveyard rats were able to kill mountain man Corey Webster, and that makes them dangerous enough to worry about."

Both men waited among the boulders, vigilant and grimly silent. Now and then a sudden gust of chilly wind wrinkled the surface of the spring. An ivory moon crept toward its zenith and the forest grew still and silent except for the soughing of wind in the pines and the distant, yipping barks of a coyote.

The snapping, sparking fire burned lower and lower, and Fargo began to wonder if he'd guessed this bunch wrong. Maybe they didn't have the oysters to sneak into the camp, meaning he and Wade would have to become ambush targets once again along a dangerous trail.

While Fargo's fancy coined these ideas, a stick suddenly snapped almost straight out ahead of them. Fargo nudged Wade to make sure he was wide awake.

Two—no, three—shadowy forms were closing in on the fire. One, Corey's four-barreled shotgun at the ready, moved far enough into the firelight for Fargo to make out a beard-smudged face and a floppy hat. Fargo shucked out his Colt and quietly drew the hammer back to full cock. Wade followed suit.

"Wait until he kills us," Fargo whispered.

Even though he knew it was coming, the roaring explosion of the shotgun made Fargo wince. An explosion of fiery pain in Fargo's chest and left arm told him that a few pellets of buckshot had ricocheted off the numerous rocks. He heard Wade hiss when some stray pellets bit him, too.

The lethal weapon's incredible blasts briefly turned night into day as the Butcher Boy rained hell on the buckskin men. The four blasts in quick succession were enough to illuminate a tall, rangy man with a hatchet-sharp profile and a huge bear of a man with blunt features—and a butcher knife in his belt.

"Take hatchet face!" Fargo ordered Wade, even as he dropped a quick bead on the intruder with the butcher knife, purposely drilling him in the left leg with a slug and dropping him.

The man with the shotgun, realizing they'd been bamboozled, dropped the weapon and began running in headlong panic. Going full bore, he tripped over a root and landed headfirst on a boulder. The neck bone snapped with a sound like green wood splitting. His body twitched like a gut-hooked fish until Fargo tossed a finishing shot into his head.

Guns drawn, the two men approached the only survivor.

Fargo bent down, drew his shooter, and tossed it aside. "Baylis Ulrick," he said in a flat, toneless voice, not making it a question. "So you're the bravo who carved up all those bodies?"

The big, bluff, flint-eyed face was ugly and defiant in the red-orange flickers of the campfire. "Yeah, Fargo, I cut up that old geezer pard of yours—cut him up into sausage stuffin's. And I carved up them bitches, too, and a few soldiers. Wha'd'you say to *that*, you crusading son of a bitch?"

"You're on a roll, Ulrick. Keep talking."

"Talk? Christ, I'm bragging. By hell, us Butcher Boys come within an ace of putting you and this titty baby under, buckskins! That rock slide was a smart play."

"You damn near left both of us flatter than a one-sided pancake," Fargo agreed. "Then again, you *almost* lived through this night. And 'almost' ain't worth a busted trace chain."

"Eat shit, preacher! All you're gonna do is shoot me clean because you're the noble Trailsman—a knight in buckskins, the ink slingers call you. You got a whatchacallit, a *code*, anh? You don't torture men."

"I am a sweet son of a buck," Fargo agreed. "And I been saving something sweet just for you—something I took from Corey Webster's shack after you boys missed it. Wade, give me a hand with old Baylis here."

Each man took one end and they hauled the big man to a spot Fargo had searched out earlier. While Wade covered him, Fargo rummaged in his saddlebags and returned with a jar and four rawhide whangs.

"The hell you up to?" Baylis demanded when Fargo used a rock to pound in the stakes. Fear had edged out the cockiness in his tone.

Fargo ignored him, tying the man spread eagle over the giant red ant colony beneath him and cutting away his clothing. The insects were not disturbed yet, but Fargo knew it wouldn't be long when he finished pouring the jar of honey all over the sick-brained killer.

"What the—? Fargo, Jesus H. Christ! The joke's gone far enough! Just buck me out with a bullet!"

Fargo used a stick to rile up the ants. "A 'code' doesn't mean anything if a man doesn't stick to it. And the oldest code in the world is the Code of Hammurabi: an eye for an eye. Or in your case, guts for guts. These ants will start with your eyeballs, and when they're finished, there'll be only a skeleton and some hair."

The first screams began soon after, hideous, inhuman shrieks that stilled the insect hum.

"Don't worry, shavetail," Fargo told Wade. "I once spied on Comanches doing this. The ants will eat the tongue and voice box quick and the screams will stop."

Fargo's prediction proved right. Soon all was silent except for the vaguely liquid sound of thousands of ants eating.

"That's not my usual gait," Fargo told Wade calmly after they had hauled the other bodies well away from camp. "But Corey Webster wasn't your usual friend, and Baylis Ulrick isn't your usual killer. I'm no plaster saint."

"I enjoyed it just fine," Wade assured him, coiling a rope around him to fend off rattlers and then rolling up in his blanket. "Now let Ulrick burn in hell."

"Just in case there is no hell," Fargo said as he pulled his hat over his eyes and rested his head on his saddle, "I gave him a taste of it on earth."

Even before the last cobwebs of sleep were swept from Fargo's eyes, he was awake and pulling on his boots. One last job remained before this puzzle was solved and the Butcher Boys case placed in the book of Santa Fe's darker history.

"Up and on the line, soldier blue," he said, kicking Wade's leg. "We got some horses to wrangle."

The early-morning sun was pale and weak, the high-altitude air still carrying a knife edge of chill. It took only a half hour of searching on foot to locate the ill-used outlaw horses. They were picketed in dense woods with no water or graze nearby.

"We'll grain and water them at our camp," Fargo decided, "then tie a lead line on 'em and take them back to Santa Fe with us."

"Think they're stolen?"

Fargo shook his head. "Those four owlhoots were already wanted, and they wouldn't likely draw more attention by boosting horses. They stole enough money from those ranchers to pay for these. Manuel was good to us, so we'll turn them over to him. With rest and a few good feeds, these will be crackerjack mounts."

Fargo was searching the saddlebags on a big claybank when he found what he was looking for—a tin box with a broken lock. It contained a sizable sheaf of papers—invoices, bills of sale, and several letters between Frank Tutt and Major Bruce Harding. Fargo sat down on a flat rock and began poring over them.

"Yep," Fargo said when he finally looked up. "Like I figured, the gang had old Red Crest dead to rights. I doubt he'll ever show his face in Santa Fe again until he's caught and brought back in a tumbleweed wagon."

"Is Harding in it, too?" Wade said in a hopeful tone.

Fargo grinned. "Up to the hubs. With these papers, the trials will be over quicker than a hungry man can eat a biscuit. It seems Harding, as procurement officer for the Third Cavalry, was placing large orders with his brother for armaments and ammunition. But the stuff was only shipped on paper—'Indian raids' kept it from reaching Santa Fe. Since the government has to honor all debts for goods duly shipped, the brother was collecting some handsome payments."

Wade loosed a whistle. "Say! Harding will spend the rest of his life in prison for that. But how does Tutt figure into it?"

"Harding dared not bank, or keep on hand, the kinds of amounts his brother was sending out. But Tutt's Gilded Cage banks a fortune every week. So the gunsmith sent his brother's share to Tutt, who collected a twenty-percent fee and parceled it out to Harding anytime he needed a little mazuma."

"Why," Wade wondered, nodding toward the sheaf of papers, "would Tutt be stupid enough to keep all this? It's incriminating as hell."

"That's exactly why he kept it—in case Harding got cold feet or tried to cut him out."

"Harding—that sanctimonious son of a bitch," Wade said. "Playing the rule book commander with me, and all the time he's a traitor to his country."

"Crooked as cat shit," Fargo agreed. "Now both of 'em are up Salt River. And since you played a hand in exposing Harding, I reckon you've got your first citation coming—and that field assignment you want."

"Maybe not. We lived like rajahs in that Dorsey House, and I went way over my per diem."

Fargo grinned. "Son, you're a hero now. And Harding will soon be wearing a ball and chain. I'll talk to Colonel Peatross, and he'll square it away."

"So you're going on that mapmaking expedition?"

"I'll have to—I'm a mite light in the pockets," Fargo said. "But first I mean to pay my respects to the lovely Leora."

"You're forgetting the reward," Wade reminded him. "I can't take it by law, but you can. Five hundred dollars."

The Trailsman shook his head. "This was personal. I don't profit off my friends."

Fargo pushed to his feet and began jerking up picket pins.

"Yeah," Wade said, "that part about Leora is all hunky-dory for you. But what else does Skye Fargo get out of it? You hauled most of the freight."

Fargo's lake blue eyes watched the young officer. "If you had ever known Corey Webster, Lieutenant, you wouldn't ask that question. By God, *there* was a man."

# LOOKING FORWARD!
## The following is the opening section of the next novel in the exciting *Trailsman* series from Signet:

## TRAILSMAN #359
## PLATTE RIVER GAUNTLET

*The sprawling prairie, 1861—*
*where hostiles and beasts drenched*
*the grass with blood.*

They were eight days out of Camp Franklyn when they came on the slaughter.

Skye Fargo was half a mile ahead of the patrol. The day before he had come on the tracks of unshod horses and now the soldiers were pushing to overtake the Indians and find out if they were friendly or hostiles.

Fargo rode with his Henry across his saddle. He was a big man, broad at the shoulders, narrow at the hips. Buckskins clad his whipcord frame. Around his neck was a red bandanna and around his waist a gun belt and a Colt. His lake blue eyes constantly roved the ground and the horizon.

Dark specks in the sky to the east drew his interest, and brought a frown. He tapped his spurs to the Ovaro and the stallion broke into a trot. The specks grew and became circling buzzards.

The prairie rose to a grassy swell that hid whatever drew the carrion eaters.

Fargo slowed to a walk and drew rein when he was near the top. Dismounting, he dropped onto his belly and snaked high enough to see.

The homestead wasn't much to brag about. A simple soddy, with a sod corral. It didn't even have a door. Only a ripped, faded piece of blanket for a curtain, torn and flapping in the wind. A body lay a few feet from the shadowed doorway, another farther around.

"Hell," Fargo said. He saw no sign of the culprits and reckoned it was safe. Rising, he snagged the stallion's reins and walked down.

Buzzards already on the ground took reluctant wing.

The homesteader had been chopped and sliced and hacked.

His wife had tried to reach the corral and their horse. She never made it.

Entering the soddy, Fargo nearly tripped over a third body. It was the daughter. She wasn't more than ten. He went back out and sat with his back to the soddy.

Flies buzzed about the pools of blood; a big one was crawling in and out of what was left of the homesteader's nose.

"Jackass," Fargo said. The man had no business bringing his family so far from anywhere. People back east couldn't seem to get it through their thick heads that the West wasn't tamed. Once they crossed the Mississippi River they left civilized life, with its laws and security, behind. Out here, the only law was be quick or be dead.

Plucking a stem of grass, Fargo stuck it in his mouth and settled back to wait. He heard the rumble of hooves and the clatter of accouterments long before the patrol came over the swell.

Lieutenant Peters sat his saddle ramrod-stiff. He looked too young to be an officer. Every night he polished his shoes and when on the move he constantly brushed dust from his uniform. Drawing rein, Peters gaped at the bodies and the flies. "My God."

"First you've ever seen?" Fargo was aware that this was the lieutenant's third patrol, ever.

"What?" Peters said absently, unable to tear his eyes from the hideous remains.

"Someone mutilated," Fargo said.

"Oh, yes." Peters swallowed and wheeled his mount. "Sergeant Rhodes, form a burial detail. We will see to these good people and then go after the savages responsible."

Rhodes was a block of muscle, a veteran of the Indian campaigns. "Yes, sir," he dutifully responded. "If you're sure that's wise, sir."

Lieutenant Peters cocked his head. "How can it not be, Sergeant? We mustn't let the perpetrators go unpunished."

"If you say so, sir," Sergeant Rhodes said, swinging down. "But you might want to talk to our scout."

Peters turned to Fargo. "What does he mean, I should talk to you? I know Colonel Danvers instructed me to heed your advice but what can you possibly say that will change my mind?"

"There are twice as many hostiles as there are of us," Fargo said.

"Yes, you already told me that. But we can't let that deter us."

"We should," Fargo said.

Lieutenant Peters sniffed. "I wouldn't have taken you for a coward. You come highly recommended. The colonel says you're one of the best."

"Then maybe you should get your head out of your ass and listen."

Some of the troopers overheard and cracked grins.

"I beg your pardon." Peters said.

"You heard me," Fargo said. "We go after them, we're asking for a massacre."

"How very dramatic of you. I assure you my men can handle three times as many savages."

"No," Fargo said. "You can't. These are Lakotas. Or Sioux, as you probably call them. Miniconjous, I suspect. Most are seasoned warriors." He gestured at the column of soldiers on horseback. "Your men are almost all green recruits. Hell, most have peach fuzz on their chins."

"We are *soldiers*," Lieutenant Peters said archly. "Professionals, I might add. We can hold our own against a bunch of unorganized primitives. We have carbines, after all, and what do they have? Bows and arrows."

"God Almighty."

"What?"

"You're so full of yourself, it's a wonder you don't burst those shiny buttons." The officer colored with resentment, and Fargo went on. "These primitives, as you call them, climbed on their first horse about the same time they learned to walk. They can ride rings around you. As for weapons, your men have Springfields. At best they can fire two or three shots a minute. A Sioux warrior can let eight arrows fly in the same amount of time."

"Enough," Lieutenant Peters said. "Do you seriously intend to sit there and advise me not to pursue the renegades who committed these atrocities?"

"You sure like big words," Fargo said. "Yes, if you know what's good for you, you won't."

"Your advice had been noted and rejected," Lieutenant Peters declared. "Now tell me. How far ahead would you say the hostiles are?"

"Not more than a couple of hours."

"Good. Mount up. We will overtake them and make them pay."

"Or be wiped out," Fargo said.